Halo Hattie and Discovery

Praise Notes:

"This is the next Shrek. The black version!"

Shabz Kariem, Comedian

"A diverse cultural melting pot of fun!"

Chantelle Gillespie, Poet

"I love it! It's so funny!"

Charlotte James, 11 years (Actress for Halo Hattie audiobook)

LA Edwards

Halo Hattie and the Galaxiers Discovery

Halo Hattie and the Galaxiers Discovery

Published by Birdy May Ltd

© 2021 LA Edwards

ISBN: 978-1-9996042-6-4

Cover Image & Photography: LA Edwards Illustrated by: Mary Ibeh
Edited by: OB Edwards

For information contact: Birdy May Ltd, The Curve, 81 Tempest Street, Wolverhampton, WV2 1AA. E-mail: halohattieteam@gmail.com

Acknowledgements

Father, I come to you in Jesus' name with my heart bowed and humble before you. I Bless your Name Lord for giving me the strength to write this book. It has all come from you God and I thank you.

Dedication

Dad & Uncle

Thank you to...

Oz

For your unwavering, unconditional love and support. You are truly a gift from God!

CONTENTS

and the Galaxiers Discovery

1
Fire-cracking, HotHot, Chilli Sizzle, Razzmatazz, Sass Crisps Plan

How many of you have had to get a job at nine years old? Well, meet Hattie. She believes she does not have a choice. To prepare for employment, Hattie gathers a loaf of bread, a packet of Fire-cracking, HotHot, Chilli Sizzle, Razzmatazz Sass crisps, and an inflatable giraffe swimming ring. Not quite sure what job she'll get with those! Well actually...on second thoughts, maybe she could be...

A busking bread juggler
or...
A gondola driver of a bread boat

Never heard of a bread boat? It's a boat made out of bread. Hattie could use such a boat to offer tours of the River Thames; although she pronounces the 'H' in Thames, it's possible no one would notice. Her last job choice could be...

A local food trader at Camden Market

She could wait until her food supplies got mouldy and then flog 'em as antiques for some pretty pennies and pounds. SWEET! Whatever choice Hattie makes, it must work, because her mission was about to begin.

Two minutes past midnight, TAP. TAP. TAP. There it was, the anticipated knock. Hattie pulled back her curtains and peered out of the window.

'Come on,' Mia beckoned to Hattie.

It was time for action. Hattie threw off her dressing gown and hurriedly secured her inflatable giraffe ring over her swimming costume. Next, she pulled on her orange duffle coat, although she had difficulty getting it over the inflatable giraffe. When she finished getting dressed, she looked puffed up in her outfit, as though she was wearing six Victorian petticoats. This seemed more obvious, particularly when she fastened the top two toggles, as the inflatable giraffe's head stuck out from under her coat, like a joey in its mother's pouch. Now, she looked like a Victorian cow (that's the name of a female giraffe by the way), holding onto a truck load of farts.

Grabbing her backpack and £3.50 in five penny pieces which she had saved up just for this venture, Hattie opened her bedroom door carefully and crept into the hallway. In that outfit, she could only waddle, as she tried to avoid the boxes marked, *'kitchen,' 'lounge' and 'mum's room.'*

She shim-toed (an awkward mix of shimmying and tiptoeing) silently through the unlit hallway towards the front door. She would be in big trouble if she was found leaving the flat, especially at night!

She turned the handle on the front door and opened it slowly, making sure not to make a sound. Her bestie Mia, was waiting at the front door of her ground floor flat. They hugged each other excitedly before walking as fast they could out of the estate, and onto the summer night streets of Islington.

The sky was dark and the night was still. Only the sound of jangling padlocks and rattling garage doors, caused by the slight breeze, disturbed the haunting silence. After scurrying around a winding street, dodging the smell of dog wee and garbage, they turned the corner into Billy Horn Alley. It was really garages in an alley where they sometimes played, but the locals renamed it, Billy Horn Alley. Apparently, a man named Billy B. Horn lives there. The story is that he has a horn growing from his head. He uses it to break into garages which makes banging noises throughout the night. If any of the garage owners were brave enough to face Billy B. Horn - although no-one knew how to, they too supposedly would end up with a horn growing out of their head!

Finally, they reached Hattie's mother's garage to collect supplies for their journey.

Mia broke the silence first. "W...W...We can't do this Hattie!" she stammered.

"We're like sisters," replied Hattie, "if we don't, I won't see you again."

Mia said, "I suppose we could get jobs as duo champion crisp sandwich eaters!"

"Yeah," Hattie smiled, "we've got enough crisps, haven't we?"

The girls knew by the next day they would be far away. Only then would the job hunt really begin. *Eeek!*

Using a spare key she had sneaked from her kitchen, Hattie fiddled with the garage padlock. Eventually, it clicked open. The girls pushed the scraggy wooden door and stepped inside. It was pitch black. Mia was scared and tried to grab Hattie's hand as Hattie fumbled to flick on the lights.

CLICK. The girls looked up and FROZE!

Sitting on a stack of boxes was Hattie's mother, Ava. On the opposite side, squeezing the life out of an old table with her, let's say, roundish thickset, was June, Mia's Auntie. The table was already heavy-laden with dried-up tins of paint and rolls of damp wallpaper and didn't need any help from Auntie June's horse-sized backside.

"MIA!" Auntie June yelped in thick patois. "There'll be no adventures at this time of night for you. Oh, and you do realise don't you, that it's popcorn night? I didn't even get to finish my garlic pickled ice cream and fish flavoured doughnut."

Auntie June fixed Mia with a wicked stare, "...and all the cheese and chicken foot flavour is probably finished by now - you know what your Uncle Miggles is like; yuh can't get a look in!"

Auntie June who was clearly missing a night to remember, showed little regard for her niece's plan to abscond with a swimming costume and a packet of bargain crisps.

She released her weight from that poor side table which wobbled and groaned on its wooden frame. Still wearing her old mangled striped tangerine nightie and matching dressing gown with her yellow furry bed slippers, she circled the girls with her hands on her hips.

"Mia June Numptie-McBrowning, I want the truth missus. Now! Did you take my jumbo pack of Fire-cracking, HotHot, Chilli Sizzle, Razzmatazz, Sass Crisps?"

Hattie cringed and reluctantly raised her index finger to admit to this inexcusable crime, as Mia had sneaked them out of her house for her. Auntie June scowled at them. All the girls could do was stare at the floor in embarrassment.

"Well?" asked Hattie's mum. "Are you going to tell us what's going on? You both know you shouldn't be out alone at night...and planning to run away? C'mon girls, you know better than that."

This question too, was met with a pin drop silence from Hattie and Mia.

Without another word, Auntie June hurriedly ushered Mia out of the garage. Hattie didn't even get to say goodbye to her. Watching them leave, Hattie knew she would never see Mia again.

2

Hatzweze's Grace

The next morning, Hattie woke up feeling sad about her failed attempt to run away with Mia. They nearly made it, but Auntie June with her crabby toes and wild ginger hair caught them at the last minute. They would be together now, in central London, setting up their new business; although it's fair to say, their career choice was debatable.

After getting dressed, Hattie grabbed her yellow 'Slay Melanin' titled journal and closed the door to her bedroom for the last time. She walked through the empty hallway and out of her flat. She was moving house today and as the last items from her home were being loaded onto the Smashing Removals van, Hattie climbed into her mum's new car. She watched as her mother Ava, locked the front door of their old flat for the final time.

By mid-afternoon, Hattie and Ava had arrived at their new home in Wembley. Her mum could now afford this new house with a garden, as she had just got a new job as a graphic designer for a global company based in central London. Although Hattie couldn't share this moment with Mia, she was still excited to see her new garden. She'd never had one before; just the eery old Billy Horn Alley. While Ava went back and forth showing the removal men where to put their belongings in their new house, Hattie jumped out of her mum's car ready to explore her new home. She started downstairs. It was open plan style. The lounge was linked to the kitchen and it had a brand new smell. A large light blue island sat in the middle with a row of high stools underneath one side, and counter space for eating. The kitchen was painted a strange purply blue colour. The sun beamed through the floor to ceiling glass windows at the opposite end. Hattie ran towards the windows and noticed they were actually concertina doors. Wow! There was so much light - it was just like being outside, but she was actually inside. This was pretty cool! She turned the lock until it clicked and slid the doors open.

She stepped out into her new garden and smiled as her Hatzweze trainers graced the garden's main path for the first time. She was wearing her favourite denim dungarees and frilly fuchsia t-shirt underneath. The garden was beautiful. She held her arms out to the side and twirled around holding her face up to the sky. The glare of the midday sun made her afro curls glisten and her brown skin glow. She tightened the yellow and white bandana around her hair and straightened her diamanté cat eye glasses. This was just what she wanted. If only she could share this moment with Mia!

Along the hedges of the garden, were rows of pink fuchsias, nestled amongst wax flowers and white perennials. The grass was freshly cut. In between the towering conifer trees at end of the garden, was an overgrown rosebush. Its peach and orange coloured petals were interwoven with thorns and winding bramble. Hattie was so happy she now had a garden to play in. She wandered a little further towards the rosebush admiring every inch of her new garden. She stopped for a moment, as she thought she could hear rustling. Hattie looked around to see where the sound came from—

"Hello pet," came a voice.

"Uh! Who said that?" Hattie gasped.

"It is I," the voice chuckled.

"W. w. w...who, who is that?" she asked, looking around eagerly.

"HERE I AM!"

Hattie noticed a bird perched on the fence.

"Did you just...spe-ak...?" Hattie asked, feeling spooked.

"Yes, I did," the bird said, smiling.

Hattie moved closer, to get a better look at the bird. It was bespectacled and slightly pudgy. It had light grey feathers and a white patch on its neck. There was a bright pink tag wrapped around one leg, and its claw nails were painted a vivid crimson.

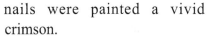

"I am Peggy Pigeon," the bird announced. "And you are?"

"B...but you're a...a...bir —" Hattie said befuddled.

"A wood pigeon, thank you VERY much," Peggy Pigeon said indignantly. She had an aversion to the word, 'bird.' She thought it sounded...well, common. Peggy Pigeon toddled closer to Hattie.

"What's your name dear?"

"Er...er...um, it's Hattie."

"Well, don't be frightened dear, all is well! Fiddlesticks, where *are* my manners? Let me welcome you to the 'Galaxy Garden.' My friends and I are resident here. We live..." she whispered, "*down there,*" gesturing with a shift of her head at the rose bush towards the bottom of the garden.

"I must show you around my home. Come dear." Peggy Pigeon said.

Before Hattie could respond, she noticed a mouse wearing pink shoes and a candy print dress appear at her feet with a humongous grin.

"My name is Missie Mouse," the mouse announced in a loud shrill. "I live under your house with my family. I'm the youngest out the lot me. I was born *right here* in the Galaxy Garden! It's my home."

Hattie backed away cautiously as the mouse continued to speak.

"I tell you what. I love to eat you know. Any food, anything, anytime, anywhere...I like things like sugar... ooooo and chips, yeahhhh, pavement chips are the best! I look for food in alllllllllllllllllllllllllllllllll the land of your house. Well, all the houses actually...hahahaha! Anyway, c'mon follow me!" the mouse bounced up and down trying to tug at Hattie's hand.

"Errrrmmm," Hattie said, unsure.

"Oh pleeeeeease Hattie, come, come, come, come, come," Missie Mouse begged. Peggy Pigeon signalled for Missie Mouse to stop. She didn't want Hattie being frightened, even though she knew Hattie would have to enter the rosebush at some point!

CLACKARACKCLACK
CLACKARACKCLACK

A loud sound came from Hattie's garden and the back gate flung open, startling Hattie. A golden horse wearing a tan leather jacket with fur collars covered in badges, sauntered through the gates. It wore gold watches around its ankles and sovereign rings around two of its hooves. It trotted towards Hattie looking like a cheap pre-decorated Christmas tree - well, a shabby-chic second-hand one at least; especially with that poor boy hat.

"Awwight? I'm 'Oward 'Orse. Pleased to meet ya kid." He said, as he chewed gum furiously, his gold tooth reflecting in the sun. He extended a hoof to shake Hattie's hand.

"I'm a Londoner me. A good 'ole East End boy. I live behind your garden and yeah, just call me ennit." His mobile phone rang. He turned away to answer it.

"Take a Butchers Entertainment Agency, what can I do you for?"

After listening to the caller, Howard Horse snapped, "I'm gonna put one right across your canister, you plonker! I told ya DJ Diggidy Dangly Duck has got suvink else on pal. Tell you what right...proper mustard deal, jus' for you though, yeah. 'Ow's about the breakdancing Afro Bees? Twenty-three sovereigns and they're *yours* bruv."

He paused, then began protesting, "NO? Are you 'avin a real Mccoy? That's a steak meal pal. Call me when you wanna talk biness, yeah!"

He winked at Hattie and trotted out the gate. Peggy Pigeon shook her head and sighed.

"I must say, you are not obliged Hattie, to provide us with food, *especially* Missie Mouse...and YOU Howard Horse," she hollered down the garden after him. "You must find a way of being more welcoming." He popped his head through the gate again while on his phone.

"Sorry kiddo. Next time though yeah...? Got a biness to run."

"Well...I'd better get back," Hattie said as she turned quickly to walk up the garden path.

"Er, wait. Er, tell me ab.. ab.. about yourself pet?" Peggy Pigeon said stumbling along the fence, trying to keep up with Hattie, "and, slow down girl, I don't like to get my nails chipped!" Peggy tittered.

"Erm...well...I'm Hattie Mae James. I'm...erm... I'm nine. My parents split up four years ago, but I still speak to my Dad. He lives in Jamaica. I'm an only child and I don't really have anyone to play with. My best friend Mia was like my sister, but now I've moved away from her, I'm going to be all on my own."

"Never mind dear. You can play with me and my friends. We all live here in the Galaxy Garden because *we* have lost our friends and families *too*. We are all trying to find them. The Galaxy Garden has been waiting."

Peggy stopped abruptly and announced, "YOU Hattie, are the new halo bearer!"

"Huh!" Hattie exclaimed. "What's that?"

"A halo? You'll wear it as a crown dear. You'll be a queen and you will have *power* in the Galaxy Garden!"

Peggy clenched her claws and puffed her chest out proudly.

3
De Nada

The next day, Hattie tried to crawl through the rosebush at the end of her garden to find the Galaxy Garden HQ. Peggy Pigeon had said she should come and meet her friends, but she couldn't find the way in.

Hattie tried to burrow her way through the dense undergrowth but it felt more like wading . through stinging nettles than entry into the Galaxy Garden HQ. It didn't help that it was hot and stuffy.

After trying several times, she was exhausted. She was about to give up when - THUD!!! She banged the crown of her head on something solid.

"Ouch!" Hattie shouted.

Her head throbbed with pain. She looked up to see what she'd hit her head on. A wall of flowers blocked her path! It was no ordinary wall. It was covered in light pink roses and towered over her, making her feel as tiny as a lego piece! The petals looked rotten and smelled like raw meat and dog farts. Urgh! Some rosebush! She didn't understand. How could she meet Peggy's friends if she was blocked by this wall? Although worn out and confused, Hattie was keen to try again. This time, she would use *all* her might. She filled her lungs with air, tensed her arms and pushed, but after three failed tries, she'd had enough. The wall of roses wasn't moving. She slumped against the flower wall causing some of the petals to crumble onto the sunbaked soil. She reached up to try and catch the desiccated florets as they trickled through her fingers.

"Right!" Hattie exclaimed. "Last try! I'm going to push this wall as hard as I can. My dad said I must always try my best." She took a deep breath in and blew the broken floret pieces out of her hands to get started.

WwwhoooossssshhhHHH

The florets dispersed into the air. Hattie watched with curiosity as the particles glistened under the sun's rays. They looked like a constellation of stars as they hung in the air, then floated dreamily, before covering the soil like icing sugar over a Victorian sponge cake. Mesmerised by their sequin charm, Hattie knelt and looked closer. Her eyes widened with excitement. She reached out her index finger to touch them and giggled, as the gold dust tickled slightly.

Ziiiiiiiiiiiiiiinnnnnnnnnnnnnnnnnnnngggggg!

Instinctively, Hattie snatched her finger back and tried to shake off what felt like an electric shock. The gold dust rose from the ground, like a swarm of bees flying in formation. It picked up speed suddenly. Hattie stood up and backed away. The dust zipped and darted through the air. It was loud and fast, whizzing into a cyclonic sandstorm. After a few seconds, it descended on Hattie, wrapping itself around her. She tried to fight it off but it wrestled her to the ground.

"Aaaaaaaaaaaaaaah," she shrieked. She became frantic and tried to escape. All she'd wanted was to play with Peggy Pigeon and Missie Mouse. Why was this happening? She rolled around on the ground, trying to set herself free but realised she couldn't.

A few seconds later, the ground began to rumble, and as it got louder, and more thunderous, Hattie's body shuddered. The soil bounced up and down as a booming sound tore through the dome.

BOOM DE BOOM, DE BOOM

RRROOOAARR!

A giant electric blue-haired rabbit with short curly platinum blonde hair, erupted ferociously from the soil. It wore a gold three-piece top and tail suit and red glitter shoes which almost blinded the sun. It was carrying an oversized blue glitter suitcase.

"Oooohhhhhhh, Hola, Hola, Hola. Lo siento. So sorry! We're very, very late!" The rabbit said as it shook off excess soil. It laid the suitcase on the ground and clicked open the locks. The suitcase transformed into an elongated table, with what looked like bric-a-brac from all nations scattered on top. The rabbit ignored the sandstorm swirling around Hattie and shouted over the incessant noise,

"MUCHO TRÁFICO ON RABBIT HOLE ROUTE Nuevo tres cinco, 935. WE'VE BEEN UP AGAINST IT TO GET HERE, *I* TELL YA. PEGGY PIGEON WILL HAVE OUR GUTS FOR GARTERS BEING THIS LATE. DON'T WORRY, HATTIE; WE'LL GET YOU SORTED. NO PROBLEM, DE NADA."

4
All Hail Her Galaxy Garden Majesty

BOOM BOOM, *BOOM DE **BOOM***

RRROOOOAAARRR

BOOM BOOM, *BOOM DE **BOOM***

RRROOOOAAARRR

BOOM BOOM, *BOOM DE **BOOM***

RRROOOOAAARRR

Three more oversized, blue-haired rabbits, wearing matching gold suits, erupted from the ground, causing astronomic craters. Surprisingly, the hole replaced itself with soil, making a loud ZWEEEP noise. The rabbits ignored the gold dust encircling Hattie, as it wrapped itself tighter around her body. Its rapid pace made it hard for her to breathe. Even though Hattie was trapped, the rabbits continued to focus on preening themselves with beautifying artefacts, laid out on the table. The array of sweet-smelling beautifiers were simply astounding:

Black seed, prickly pear and avocado body oil
Courgette, cucumber and goosegrass deodorant
Sweetcorn toothbrushes with aloe vera toothpaste
Pumpkin seed and dill eyebrow shaper
Fuchsia and dahlia párfum
Oat and blackberry leaf fur exfoliator
Mint and rosemary breath freshener

One Rabbit who seemed to be having a love affair with a breath freshener, skipped towards Hattie. He put the breath freshener in one pocket and from the other pocket, he pulled out a yellow honking hooter which had a rubber toot on its end. He was wearing a stunning red tie labelled, 'Raymundo - Wonder Warren HQ Porter.' He stood over Hattie as she tried to untangle herself.

Raymundo squeezed the rubber toot once. A neon pink tongue the length of the Eiffel Tower, BURST OUT of the hooter. The tongue was full of salvia bubbles which dripped all over Hattie. Each time he squeezed the toot, the tongue popped out of the horn thingy and sucked up more of the gold dust storm, swirling around Hattie.

ZOOP!

ZOOP!

ZOOP!

Finally, Hattie was free! She coughed, spewing gold dust from her lungs. She was exhausted. Relieved, she sat up, trying to catch her breath and began to brush gold dust from her clothes. Humming lightly and on the tip of his toes, Raymundo circled Hattie. He repeatedly squeezed the rubber toot, which helped to remove the remaining dust from her hair.

Meanwhile, the other three rabbits, unfolded a magnificent white velvet chaise lounge. The rim was elaborately decorated with gold Grecian patterns. It was arranged with the finest gold cushion, adorned with the letter "H" in the centre.

The four rabbits then surrounded Hattie, lifted her up and placed her onto the chaise lounge. They hoisted it carefully onto their shoulders. One rabbit held each corner. They stood like soldiers with one arm behind their backs. Hattie didn't have a potato waffle what was going on now!

"Erm, excuse me," enquired Hattie, "are you guys taking me home?"

"Hola, hello," one rabbit whispered to Hattie, "señorita, er, Miss Hattie," he raised one furry finger to his pitted lip and whispered, "ssssshhhh," then turned to face the wall of roses.

DUH DUH DUH DUH DUH

DDDUUUUUUUHHHHH!

Sounded a symphony of horns and timpani. In unison, the rabbits faced the wall of roses. They stood there for a moment, before the wall slowly rose upwards. Smoke rose from the ground and streaming gold pyros descended like fireworks enveloping and shaping into an archway. Roses sprang into bloom, each petal unfolding, turning from pink to ruby red. Above the archway, emblazoned in yellow and red Queen of the Night flowers, was a sign which read,

'GALAXY GARDEN.'

In unison, the rabbits announced:

"ALL HAIL HER GALAXY GARDEN MAJESTY,

HATTIE MAE JAMES...."

5

Discotheque Discovery

Behind the archway, a roaring party was in session.

Hattie stared in amazement at the spectacle she was witnessing. The Galaxy Garden opened up into a vast dome-shaped stadium. There was a ginormous 'WELCOME' sign hanging from a large oak tree in the middle of dome. It was labelled, 'Galaxy Tree' with a Treehouse on its right hand side.

The walls of the dome were made out of intertwined rose stems with two gigantic doorways on either side. The sign over one doorway read, *'Galaxy Galley'* and over the other, *'Galaxy Bathrooms'* and two others were labelled, *'Galaxy Music Room' and 'Galaxy Gallery.'*

Above them, were several doors curved in the shape of the dome. Names were displayed on each door and winding staircases on either side led to what looked like bedrooms with balconies. The grounds were immaculately manicured and the sun lit up all corners of the dome.

Monkey puzzle trees lined the inner corners of the dome, between neatly planted zwartkops, giant peace lilies and wax flowers. A huge cascade water feature set on a giant rock, was positioned behind the Galaxy Tree. The water constantly flowed from its fountain, spraying elegantly into the air and falling like light rain from cumulus clouds. Behind the fountain, was a gigantic oval wooden table with mounds of food expertly laid out. Bunting and a zillion balloons floated in abundance. It was truly a spectacle to behold!

Hattie was paraded on the chaise lounge through the Galaxy Garden as hundreds of animals and insects clambered over the rabbit porters to greet her and take photos. Hattie could only see some of them; there were:

Green Shield Bugs
Oxford Sandy and Black Pigs Nightjars
Pond Skaters
Buff-tailed Bumblebees Feral Goats
A Willow Warbler

Emperor Dragonflies Tamworth Pigs
A flock of Galway Sheep
Garden Tiger Moths
Connemara Ponies
Blue Faced Leicesters
Barnevelder Chickens
Red Foxes
Marmalade Hoverflies
Belted Galloways
One Hackney Horse
Chiffchaffs
Mice
Painted Lady Butterflies and one Natterjack Toad.

The Natterjack Toad was standing next to the Blue Faced Leicesters and seemed to be taking photos of Hattie's entrance. The camera light flashed several times but Hattie noticed something strange. The Toad's camera faced the wrong way. It looked like he was taking photos of something else but Hattie couldn't tell what.

Animals kept appearing from every bush, tree, and hole in the ground. Although she had no clue what was happening, Hattie smiled coyly and greeted them all.

"Yes, Hello..."

"Hi Hattie, we're The Mice Boys..."

"Hi Hattie, we're Antsy Ants..."

"Yes, Hattie, nice to meet ya, we're the Chuffing Chiffchaffs..."

"Nice to meet you..."

Although Hattie was still unsure what being a Queen of the Galaxy Garden meant, she could not believe that she had found so many new friends.

6
PING! Tiiiizzz, AAAHHH!

POOF!

Hattie was suddenly thrust onto the ground and everyone dissolved into gold dust! Only the furniture and flowers remained. There was so much dust floating in the air that she had to squint to see properly. She clambered off the chaise lounge onto the Great Galaxy Table and looked up.

"It's getting brighter," she said.

The sun turned from yellow to white. It got bigger and brighter and BRIGHTER and BIGGER. Gradually, it moved closer like a spaceship preparing to land, bringing with it, gusts of wind. It charged through the Galaxy Garden, like a windstorm. Hattie tried to keep her balance as she looked at the blazing beacon of light. She watched as an aubergine colour encircled the sun. Its colossal glow was surrounded by stars. It hovered in the air, pulsating and dazzling with the most vibrant luminosity. Then...

SNAP!

The Galaxy Garden was engulfed in darkness. Hattie was terrified. She closed and opened her eyes a few times, hoping that this was a horrible dream. But it wasn't! After a few moments, she heard a faint noise that sounded like bells. Even though it was pitch black, Hattie squinted to see if there was anyone else in the Garden. There was no-one. The faint noise gradually became louder. Hattie looked towards the sky and noticed small glimmers of light, flashing like lasers. Hattie watched in awe, as multi-coloured stars rotated through the air. They got closer and closer to Hattie. Sounding like a slot machine, they plunged downwards,

P

Pi, Pi

P. PIN

PING!

Uh oh! Something landed at the foot of the Galaxy Tree. Hattie remained still. She stared in wonderment as smoke began to rise from the base of the tree. Warily, she crawled the length of the table towards the shiny object, hung her head over the edge and stared at it. She was mesmerised by a round golden metal piece. It looked like a royal circlet, as it lay incandescent against the tree. It sparkled and sizzled, as if it was overheating. The rim of the circle was encrusted with golden pearls. A cluster of effervescent reds, striking yellows and daring purples, radiated from the ethereal jewels. The dome was now illuminated by gemstones, and the ground was the deepest hue of aquamarine that looked like multicoloured corals swaying underwater. It was magnificent!

Hattie reached out and carefully picked up the golden circle. Turning it over, she observed its enchanting shine and brilliance.

"Uh oh!" She gasped. Her hands began to spark like fireworks. She dropped the circlet and tried to get rid of the sparks by shaking her hands.

"Go away sparkles," she cried out. The firing lights from her hands began to burn the HQ greenery. Pockets of flowers were now on fire! The flames started to rise higher and higher, spreading to the monkey puzzle trees.

"Oh no," she shrieked. "The plants are dying!" Tiiiizzzzz! Another hedge was on fire. Tiiiizzzz, and another rose. Hattie stood in the middle of the dome, surrounded by an unruly fire which was started by the sparks from her hands. The ground was sizzling hot, almost scalding the soles of her trainers.

"Aaaaahhhhhh," screamed Hattie.

"Well done, my dear. You have passed the test!"

"Who's that?! What test?!" She looked around, desperate to see who spoke.

"You didn't return home, Hattie. You showed great courage and pressed forward. You passed the test with flying colours, or, should I say firing colours hahaha," the voice chuckled.

"But, the soil is melting! The flowers are on fire," Hattie yelped.

"It'll all grow back dear," the voice said calmly. Hattie looked around the dome frantically, as she could hear the voice but see no-one.

"Peggy Pigeon, is that you?" Shouted Hattie.

"Well, of course dear, no one else here speaks the Queen's English and keeps their nails looking *this* good," chuckled Peggy.

Hattie felt a gentle tap on her neck. She looked round. Peggy Pigeon was sitting on her left shoulder.

"Why did you leave me Peggy?" Hattie asked solemnly. "You said I would meet your friends and we could play together. How can I make friends now? Look at my hands!"

"Don't worry, love. It'll wear off and everything will become clear."

Peggy Pigeon rested her head against Hattie's to comfort her. Hattie snuggled in for a moment, then, stepped back abruptly, causing Peggy Pigeon to lose her balance.

"The gold ring! Oh no! Where's the gold ring? It's gone, Peggy. It's gone!" Hattie searched desperately for it, burning more shrubbery with her sparking hands.

"Girl, I nearly got my nails chipped when you stumbled like that. Anyway, calm down, dear. The gold ring you saw Hattie, *was* the halo. It'll be back," she said reassuringly, "...and stop that," she ordered.

Hattie stopped searching and slumped back on the ground. Peggy flew onto Hattie's knees, took her hands in her wing and gently blew.

WHHHHOOOOOOOSHHHH!

Peggy smiled and said, "there you are dear."

Hattie watched in amazement as the sparkles dispersed from her hands. The fires gradually became smaller and the air felt much cooler.

"Now," Peggy Pigeon said looking Hattie straight in the eye. "Hattie, my love. You *must* keep the Galaxy Garden a *secret*."

7
Stop Talking Missie Mouse!

"Hattie, Hattie, wake up. It's time for breakfast. I can smell toast. It's a bit burnt, but it'll do. Your mum's making breakfast. Come on, GET UUUPPPP!"

"Ohhh," Hattie groaned, still half asleep. She rubbed sleep from her eyes and shouted,

"Missie Mouse! What are you doing in my room? How did you get in?"

"Well..." smirked Missie. "I have my ways. Anyway, to save you coming to the Galaxy Garden, I thought I would come to you," Missie announced triumphantly. "Now, let's get breakfast. C'mon, c'mon, c'mon!"

"Peggy Pigeon said yesterday I don't need to give food to *anyone*? Don't you remember, Missie?"

"But I've brought my faaaaamilyyyy," Missie Mouse pleaded turning on her cute baby charm. Hattie leaned forward, peering over the end of her bed. There were 50 of them! All dressed in swanky dresses and smart suits. They stared expectantly at Hattie. She was almost sure some of them mouthed, 'feed me, feed me.'

"See?" Missie continued in a melancholic tone, "they're all very, *very* hunnnngry. It's just some toast."

Hattie felt sorry for them. So, she jumped out of bed and lead the mice to the kitchen and waited until her mum went to another room. Before Hattie knew it, she had a Euston Station waiting area under her kitchen table. It was overcrowded and annoyingly screechy.

"Ssshhh. Please be quiet, ok? My mum will find out if you're too noisy, but you will be alright down there, won't you?"

"Uuummmmm, actually, NO," sneered a group of ten mice in unison. "We do not appear to have *any* napkins, cutlery, or *even* plates. How is one to enjoy a *banquet* without the required implements. You haven't even given us food, young lady! Don't you know the basics?"

"A banquet?" Hattie asked, surprised. "I don't know what a banquet is, Mr Mice, but I'm getting the food now."

"HA....... HAR........HA.......DI ......HAR." The ten mice laughed in unison. "*First* of all, you must learn our name. We are 'The Mice Boys,' famous jazz singers.

Secondly, *darling*, a banquet is a selection of high-quality foods served in luxurious surroundings. Under the table was *not* what we had in mind. I suppose you are new to this, so we'll just have to make do."

Hattie quickly busied herself trying to find some breakfast for the mice because she had to go shopping with her mum that morning. She managed to find...

* Kitchen paper towels
* Thin cheese biscuits
* Slices of bread
* Leftover eggs and bacon
* A jar of sugar
* Foil and a biscuit tin

A few hours later, Hattie returned from her shopping trip and while her mum was unpacking the car, Hattie ran ahead to check on the mice. When she looked under the kitchen table, she gazed in disbelief.

The underside of her kitchen table had been transformed into a 5-star restaurant. A crystal chandelier hung from above, warmly lighting up the space. Purple velvet draping hung from all sides of the table, and the floor glistened like white marble. An elegant mirror effect dining table filled the area (they used Hattie's biscuit tin to make this). The mice sat on chairs made from thin cheese biscuits. They'd used rolled up kitchen foil, to create Queen Anne chair legs, and using toothpicks and glass fragments, they made three-level tiered plates which rested as centrepieces on the tables, displaying, bite-size hors d'oeuvres:

- Ackee and saltfish in breadfruit baskets
- Country ham and pickle crostini with parmesan shavings
- Coco bread with escovitch fish, onions and peppers
- Mini herb frittatas with goat's cheese and smoked salmon
- Spiced bun with a selection of fine cheese
- Bite-size toast with ginger jam

Although she did not think they saw her, the Mice Boys were tapping wine glasses with toothpicks, shaking sugar in foil like maracas, clicking their fingers, and singing a fast-paced jazz song:

"Peggy P, she don't know, know, know

We gotta party like oh, oh, oh
I know, I know our flaws are like, woah, woah, woah
But we love good food, so let's go!
In the end we'll be happy like oh, oh, oh
Hope she don't find out on the low
If she does, run out the front door
Till then, let's party yeah, go, go, go! Oh!"

"Missie? Missie? Are you here?" Yelped Hattie, as she crouched under the table.

The mice were mousing around, dancing, eating and socialising. This was definitely *not* just a bit of toast. Hattie felt a tap on her shoulder. It was Missie Mouse with a twinkle in her eyes. She announced,

"THIS IS A MICE

BANQUET Hattie. Welcome to the party!"

Missie whipped out her diary and said, "I wonder if we can book another—"

"*AAAAHHHHHH*"

everyone screamed.

The kitchen table began to wobble and The Mice Boys stopped singing and looked up. The music ceased and all the mice froze. Hattie looked up.

"Peggy!" Hattie bellowed.

"Good afternoon Hattie." Peggy frowned as she landed on the kitchen table.

"I was at home taking a nap, when I was awoken by Neville the Natterjack Toad. He informed me that a Mice Banquet was in full session. I know who's responsible for this."

Neville the Natterjack Toad, sneered at Hattie as he stood next to Peggy Pigeon. He was the Galaxiers' accountant and Peggy's right-hand man. Didn't he know it! His brown warty skin gave Hattie the creeps. Eeewwww!

Peggy Pigeon flew down from the top of the table with Neville on her back and positioned herself in the centre of the Mice Banquet.

"OH NO!" Squeaked the mice in unison.

"OH YES, fellow banqueters! I see you're having another shindig," Peggy said sternly. Missie Mouse tried to hide behind her uncle's uncle's uncle's back.

"I can see you, Missie Mouse!" Scowled Peggy Pigeon. "I know this is down to you pestering Hattie. Allllllllllllllllllllllllll you mice are not in Buckingham Palace anymore. The Great Mice Oppression forced you out. That's why you are HERE!"

"These decorations...?" Peggy questioned, "this food...? I don't believe this! You've been back to the Palace, haven't you? You mice have stolen again, HAVEN'T YOU?" Peggy toddled to the table overflowing with food and started inspecting it, lifting plates and eyeing the food. She frowned, then shrieked, "did you raid Hattie's mum's cupboards as well? Goodness me! First you steal the halo, the Queen's pride and joy, and we're in enough trouble with that as it is, and now this? That's it! Galaxy Garden meeting, 6pm tonight. SHARP!"

Peggy Pigeon, Hattie and Neville the Natterjack left the Mice Banquet. The mice stood still, mouths wide open, with only the whites of their eyes shifting from side to side. Missie Mouse stepped out from behind her uncle's uncle's uncle's back and tittered,

"Did you see that, guys? She completely ignored our marble floor. We worked really hard on that!" (It was really sugar from a jar, sprinkled on the floor, in Hattie's kitchen)

All the mice shuddered and shouted,

"STOP TALKING MISSIE MOUSE."

8
Galaxiers' Cabinet Meeting

It was 5.55pm. The air was one of anticipation. The animals and insects chattered as they found their seats at the Great Galaxy Table. Even though it was an early summer's evening, the sky was clear blue with a few sparse clouds. It still felt like midday.

200 Poly Pits were carved into the surface of the Great Galaxy Table, which looked like a patchwork quilt. The pits were made from tree branches and yellow dandelion petals. Each pit had a doc leaf flag, imprinted with the surnames of Galaxiers.

The Galaxy chairs were made from dark brown and green twining, with the names of the bigger boned animals engraved on the backs of the chairs. The Table was so big that it could fit fifty chairs underneath it.

Everyone was dressed in formal attire. Hattie noticed The Mice Boys however, arriving with towels over their shoulders. They wore black mankinis, gold bow ties and goggles, clearly disregarding the dress code. Hattie asked them from across the table "why is your pit different from everyone else's?"

In unison, they replied, "this darling is a Jacuzzi, NOT a pit! We need this after a long day of performing and signing autographs. Don't you *knoooooow* who we are? We are famous!"

Before Hattie could reply, Peggy Pigeon arrived. It was exactly 6pm. She was wearing a red velvet shawl with *Galaxy Garden Gaffer* stencilled on the back. Taking her position at the head of the Great Galaxy Table, she commanded,

"HERE, HERE. You will come to order. Order!" Everyone quietened, settling into their seats.

"No doubt you will be aware of the reason for this emergency meeting. There are three matters on the agenda for discussion:

1.   Welcome
2.   Unauthorised Mice banquet
3.   Gartoid Manderblythen

Let's start by welcoming, once again our new halo bearer." Peggy Pigeon looked proudly at Hattie before extending her claws and announcing,

"Her Galaxy Garden Majesty, Hattie Mae James."

Everyone cheered as Hattie walked towards Peggy. Suddenly, two chicken security guards in sunglasses abruptly blocked her path. They were conjoined chicken twins. Their feathered chests were puffed up like body builders, and their arms, the size of blue whales, tested the stitching on their shared bomber jacket.

Bronson, in a Brummie accent said, "you can't pass this point, bab. Need to run some checks first, yeah?"

Bruiser, the other chicken, clicked his bluetooth, and replied, "well....? Whadaya fink Bronson? Is she barmy? She's got a face as long as Livery Street?"

Silence.

Bronson replied, "yeah, yeah, looks like 'er. She's got a right cob on."

"It's me," Hattie pleaded.

The chickens looked at each other and in unison said, "fair nuff luv, 0121 and do one," then stepped aside.

As soon as Hattie sat next to Peggy Pigeon, the blue sky steadily turned to an aubergine colour, forming an enlarged ring around the sun. Hattie knew what this meant from yesterday's events. Everyone stood up and peered into the sky in wonderment. This time, thunder struck and BOOMED, splitting the clouds with bolts of lightning. The sound tore through the dome. Rotating multicoloured lights fell from the sky and soared towards the Galaxy Garden, jangling like a slot machine. There it was again, the luminous halo. Its pearly rim glistening brighter than midnight stars. It burst through the dome ceiling, moving closer to the Great Galaxy Table. Eventually it slowed, hovering over Hattie's chair. The Galaxiers beamed with delight. Peggy Pigeon smiled, pleased that the halo had found its new wearer. She gestured to everyone to be seated.

"Fellow Galaxiers..." Peggy began. "I am disappointed by this morning's shenanigans. The unauthorised Mice Banquet in Hattie's kitchen? *Unacceptable!* Let me remind you of the rules. Do NOT ask Hattie for food, OR to host any more parties. Why? Well, if her mother, *or* the neighbours find out about us, they will contact the RSPCA to rescue us and place us with strangers in new homes. If that happens, they will not only destroy our HQ, but they will separate us. Or *worse*, leave us to be gawped at in zoos and to rot in farms across the country. We've managed to evade detection for nearly a year, so please, let's not be careless and put our livelihood in jeopardy.

Our mission is to locate our families from whom we've

been separated. The halo will enable Hattie to help us. WE BELIEVE IN HATTIE, DON'T WE?"

The Galaxiers cheered.

"Now, due to the unsolicited Mice Banquet, a senior member of our team has flown in from Germany to reinforce the rules. I give you....the Honourable...Dr. Gertrude Vynegarr, the Goose. Remember Galaxiers? Her name is pronounced, VINEgar."

Dr. Vynegarr, who was seated next to Peggy Pigeon, stood up. She was wearing a red frilly belly top and brown lederhosen shorts, with D.G.V. engraved on both sides of the braces. She spoke with the strangest high-pitched shrill.

"Goot avenin Galaaaaxiers. I am pleased to-a be-a here-a in your-a country. I agree with Feggy Fee. We musta keep our mission in mind all ze time. We have been able to survive in Hamburg frecisely vecause of our vigilance!"

Silence.

"Yeah, yeah. Whatever, Vinegar," a voice heckled. The meeting instantly erupted into laughter, with some animals rolling on their backs in hysterics.

"Want any salt and vynegar crisps?" Another voice yelped.

"Vinegar on your chips?" shouted another.

"Who sez zat?" Snapped Dr. Vynegarr, as her eyes bulged to the size of kiwis and her ginger-coloured beak hit the table.

"Would you like some red vine...we mean red wine?" The Mice Boys shouted in unison as they tittered between themselves.

"Order! Order I say!" hollered Peggy Pigeon.

Everyone was out of their seats rolling on the ground, crying with laughter.

"ORDER. ORDER" Peggy bellowed. They all ignored her.

" 'Ows about a lil bit of balsamic Doctor?" Howard Horse chipped in, "comes from grape VINES that does." He collapsed in uncontrollable laughter. Peggy stood up on the table to get the Galaxiers' attention.

"Silence!" she demanded.

"Hold on Peggy," Missie said, out of breath from laughing, "I've got one more. Let me get it out, let me get this out, because every time the Doctor comes here, she can't catch a break. Gertrude Prime vinegar, she's in a right pickle. Hahahaha."

The Galaxiers looked like a pack of laughing hyenas. Poor Dr Vynegarr, she'd sat down promptly, banging the table to defend her name the whole time.

"My name is pronounced, Vyne-Garr, V-I-N-E-G-a-r-r, NOT vinegar. It's pronounced Vine-garrrrrrrrrrrrrrrrrrr!" She repeated.

"ORDERRRRRRR!!!!" Yelled Peggy.

There was silence for a moment, followed by a few bouts of quiet sniggering.

Watching the animals and insects having fun, reminded Hattie of how much she missed her friend Mia.

Since moving into this house yesterday, so much had happened. She'd met talking animals, was crowned a halo bearer, sat at the head of a table at a raucous cabinet meeting, and yet she still felt alone.

"You will show respect to Dr. Gertrude Vynegarr, Galaxiers," Peggy Pigeon hollered.

"She's flown all the way from Hamburg to be here." Peggy turned to Dr. Vynegarr to apologise, then continued, as the laughter quelled.

"Right. Let's quickly move on. Next on the agenda, is the matter of Gartoid Manderblythen. He and his vagabonds are still trying to capture the halo. For six months now, they've tried without success. We are all still at risk of an attack, including Hattie. Although the brainless blue tits are following his every move, PLEASE, remain vigilant!

Right, since we've addressed the main issues, I now draw this meeting to a close; unless there is any other business."

Amidst the continued chuckling, Hattie realised she didn't like being an only child, nor did she want to be a halo bearer. She wanted to find a new best friend - someone human.

9

Scratchbum-Evans Hall Hire

Aweek after the Galaxy Garden HQ meeting, Hattie started at her new school, Wemblish Primary. Although the Galaxiers were her new friends, she was still hoping to find at least one human best friend. She'd met her new next door neighbour, Shanti and her two Golden Retrievers. Although Shanti seemed nice, she was only 6 years old and far too young to be Hattie's best friend.

She tried to make friends during PE lesson, but that ended early, as David 'Joker' Johnson released a stink bomb in the gym. Lunchtime was a social occasion for those who knew each other, but Hattie didn't like school dinners. Besides, all the pupils who brought packed lunches didn't eat them anyway; they just threw them in the bin preferring to play outside instead.

She tried to make friends in assembly, as all the year groups were together; so there was more chance of meeting someone. Except, she couldn't talk to anyone; because it was always quiet time. Hattie's last hope was to make friends with someone in the playground, but that didn't work either. So, she decided to take drastic measures.

She put up an advert on the school message board and persuaded her maths teacher, Mr Scratchbum-Evans to book the school hall for 'best friend auditions.'

On the Thursday evening of her second week after school, Hattie had prepared her interview questions and was ready for the auditions. She was seated in the hall behind an old science desk.

It was exactly 4pm. She rang the portable bell for the first auditionee to come in.

"Hello," Hattie said with a warm smile.

"Hola," the girl replied. She was tall with dark brown curly hair and light brown eyes.

"Oh hi," Hattie said, unsure. "How old are you?"

"Neuve años."

"Hmmm? What's your name?" Hattie asked.

"Me llamo Luciá, como te llamas?"

"What does that mean?" Hattie asked.

"Que?"

"What does that mean?" Hattie asked again.

"Que?"

"Do you speak any English at all?"

"Sí."

"See, what?" Hattie asked.

"Sí,sí,sí..." the girl said excitedly.

"What do you see?" Hattie asked again.

"Sí, I...er...en inglesa, pequeño, little."

"You see ....errrr....glaze?"

"Sí.......ummmm....little," Luciá nodded.

"You see, little glaze...?" Hattie asked, thinking they had found some common ground at last.

"Sí, sí," the girl smiled as if Hattie understood.

"LUCIÁ? LUCIÁ?" cried a voice from outside the hall. A middle-aged woman with long afro hair burst into the hall.

"There you are," the woman sounded relieved. She took Luciá by the hand.

"Sorry about that. Luciá is a Spanish exchange student and I lost her in the loo."

"In the loo...?" Hattie was confused.

"Well, no, not in the loo, in the loo. I meant that I went to the loos, and she wondered off from the loos."

"Oh" Hattie said, "so you both went to the loo, but she didn't go into the loo, but you went in the loo, and when you came out, she wasn't in the loos."

"Exactly," said the woman. "See ya." She said as she walked out of the hall clutching Luciá.

Hattie shouted, "wait! What's a little glaze?"

"Lucía was trying to say, she speaks little English, inglesa is Spanish for English," the woman bellowed as she left the hall.

Hattie was confused. "So, what was she trying to see?"

"Sí means yes, in Spanish," replied the woman.

"Oh, I see. Luciá was saying yes, the English are little," exclaimed Hattie.

Hattie rang the bell again. Another girl with blonde braids walked in.

"Hello," Hattie said smiling.

"Hello Hattie." The girl replied.

Hattie asked, "what year are you in?"

"I'm in the last year. I leave in a few weeks to go to Humphries Grammar School."

"Ooooo. So, what's your name and why do you want to be my friend?" Asked Hattie.

"Well, I'm Precious-Lilli, and I don't really!" She said miserably.

"Huh?"

"Well, I don't really want a new friend. I'm too intelligent to be friends with someone younger than me. Do you know I'm the most talented in the whole school?"

"Oh," Hattie said glumly. "But I'm looking for a best friend."

"My mum said I should say hello to new children at school, so I've done my bit. See ya, Hatsbe."

"But...but, my name is Hattie."

"Whatever! Toodles Hatsbe. Oh, by the way... Hatzwee, I'm the greatest tongue painter in the world and I do it to music, all on my own." She stuck out her long paint-stained tongue.

"You won a talent show with that?" Hattie laughed.

"Are you laughing at me, Hatzwee?"

"Yeah, it's funny. Why haven't you been on the telly then?"

"I'm going to be ACTUALLY."

"Yeah, what's that going to be on, Tongue's Got Talent?" Hattie laughed again.

"Yeah, you won't be laughing when all the TV

people want to sign me up to be the best tongue painter in the world...will you Hatsbe? Will you Hatsbe...?" With that, Precious-Lilli stormed out of the hall.

Although Hattie was sad that Precious-Lilli didn't want to be her friend, she had found the next big star after all. Might be considered a win-win.

Hattie rang the bell for the next auditionee. This time, a boy with spiky hedgehog hair walked in.

"Hello," he said politely.

"Hi," Hattie replied.

Hattie heard a cracking sound. *Click-crack.* She looked up to see if it would repeat. It didn't.

"So, what's your name, and why do you want to be my friend?"

"I'm Dan. I'm 10, and I want to be your friend because my dad taught me to be friends with sad lonely people."

Click-crack. Click-crack. There was that sound again. Hattie couldn't tell where it was coming from.

"Lonely, sad people?" Questioned Hattie, trying to ignore the annoying sound.

"Well yeah, that's you ent it? You're on your tod ent ya?"

"Ummm, I do have classmates, but I'm looking for a best friend. Someone I can play with after school."

"Same difference, ennit?" he said with a snarl.

Hattie noticed that Danny was curling his fingers into his palm, and cracking each finger. That's what was making that horrible sound.

"No." she said. *Click-crack* - there it was again.

"It's." *Click-crack*

"Not." *Click-crack*

"The same." *Click-crack*

Hattie had to stop after every word. The sound was so annoying.

"To." *Click-crack*

"Me." *Click-crack*

"It." *Click-crack*

"Is." *Click-crack, Click-crack.* He replied seemingly oblivious to the cracking noise.

"Danny, what are you doing with your fingers?" Shouted Hattie.

"What?" *Click-crack.* "You mean with my fingers?" *Click-crack. Click-crack.*

"I'm just cracking the joints," Danny said

jovially. The sound was atrocious. Hattie knew she couldn't possibly be friends with someone who had such an annoying habit.

"I can teach you how to do this if you want..." Danny ventured.

"Er, I'll let you know, Danny."

"No probs. Hats..." He picked up his school bag and left, this time cracking his toes. *Click-crack, click-crack*, as he walked out of the hall. Hattie rang the bell again but no-one else came in.

10

"Gordon Bennett"

A week after the failed best friend auditions, Hattie sat in her mum's shiny new 4x4 white Land Rover. She was going to drive back to Islington to see her best friend Mia. It wasn't the same speaking to her on a video call. Although she had never driven a car before, Hattie thought it looked easy, except now, she felt nervous. She swallowed the largest piece of spit she could and pressed the car's start button.

BEEP BEEP BEEP BEEP BEEP

A loud sound came from inside the car. A red-light kept flashing and, 'Parking Brake On' appeared on the dashboard.

BEEP BEEP BEEP BEEP BEEP

The sound continued. Hattie panicked and began pressing every button on the dashboard to stop the incessant noise but nothing worked. She began to sweat. Her hands felt clammy and began to tremble. She checked around anxiously to see if anyone was watching. She looked to her left. There was no one around. Then, she looked out of the driver's side window and gasped. Howard Horse was standing next to the car. He beckoned Hattie to wind the window down.

"What's your game? You're doin' my nut right in with this racket."

"I miss my best friend Mia you know, she lives by my old flat. It's only 33 minutes and 42 seconds away," she continued.

"Gordon Bennett! Do you wanna get nicked? You wally! Press that button there." Hattie pressed the STOP button and the beeping ended.

"*Doh ray mi...*you can't drive a car pal, that's taking liberties," Howard Horse said rolling his eyes. "Before I get grassed up by one of your neighbours, coz they'll think I'm a stray 'orse, I'm gonna take ya to Mia's gaff meself, 'ows about that?"

"I'd like that," Hattie said. She ran back into the house and put the car keys back exactly where she found them. She rushed back outside, ready to go to Mia's flat.

Howard Horse trotted at a gentle pace through the streets of London with Hattie on his back. He sniffed and snarled at the smell of street food and exhaust fumes in the air. When they got to Tokyngton Recreation Ground, Hattie bought some ice cream and they both sat down.

"You know what 'Attie, I miss my family as well, you know," Howard said, extending his tongue the length of the ice-cream cone and slurping the drippings.

"Where are they?" Asked Hattie.

"Dunno, pal."

"Have you looked for them?" She asked again.

Howard Horse tutted and said under his breath, "course I 'av. Gordon Bennett. Bet you've neva 'eard of travellers 'av ya? Well, my lot are Irish travellers. Yeah, originally from Ireland, but they moved 'ere. Eventually, me family settled in East London and that's where I was born. You probably don't 'av a Willy Wonka 'bout this, but we lived in caravans on sites and parks, you know. Some legal but others, well, we'd take liberties and stay on a bit of land, just for a couple of nights, mind. Can't tell ya the number of times we got moved on. I 'ated that."

"Can't you just stay wherever you find a nice park? Like here?" Asked Hattie.

"Not exactly treacle. Technically, you need a permit from the council. Anyways, one day, they turned up on our turf with a flipping court order. They had the right 'ump telling us to move on. All me family was rushed about, packing...panicking. I 'ad four older siblings, a sister and three brothers. Me parents piled them in the 'orse carriage to leave. Then, it was my turn to get in. Remember 'Attie, I was only a bab, toddler right, but me mum couldn't fit me in. *Couldn't fit me in!* Would you believe it? I was slim Jim then, I was. They should've squeezed me in like a baby in a manger, but it was over the weight limit for 'orse carriage regs. Me mum, Gord Bless 'er, tried to organise another carriage for me but the police wouldn't wait. The police told 'em, leave this baby geezer 'ere overnight, come back in the morning to get 'im, and everyfing will be sweet as a nut.

But I saw them 'Attie, I saw the police warn me parents. They said they're calling the RSPCA if they didn't come back first thing in the morning to get me. Imagine right, me...the bab, youngest out the lot, left on a piece of land tied to a ruddy lamppost. As it turns out, I didn't wait for 'em, 'Attie. I was offski, mate. I wasn't 'anging about for the RSPCA to get 'old of me reins. No mucking about, I was off.

At the time mind, me, and me family 'ad our own gaff down Brick Lane market; we worked together as brokers for 'orse racing. 'Ad our own stall and everyfink. So, I went to work the next day, 'oping that me family would come. I stayed there for a month 'Attie, but no-one turned up. I ended up shutting it down swift tidy, coz I couldn't earn as much money without the rest of me family."

"So what are you gonna do now?" Hattie asked.

"I need to stop off and get some biness done 'ere."

"No, I mean to find your family."

Howard Horse shrugged and said, "dunno kiddo...they probably went back to find me but obviously I'm 'ere now; they won't find me at the Galaxy Garden, that's all 'ush 'ush ain't it? And, as I don't know where they are. We'll probably never find each other. I guess this 'alo biness is my only 'ope. Come on treacle, let's go."

Hattie climbed onto Howard Horse's back and he galloped at great speed until they reached a small cheese and wine cafe called, 'Vinnie's Cheese Bites.' Howard knocked on the back door with his hoof. After a brief wait, the metal door opened slowly.

"Welcome-a," squeaked a voice with a strong foreign accent.

Hattie looked towards her feet and saw a dark grey mouse with white patent shoes standing at the door. He was wearing a light blue double-breasted jacket and trousers to match. A silver striped handkerchief was tucked in his breast pocket and a silvery-white cravat was stylishly arranged at his neck. The cravat had embroidery on the top, which read, 'Vincent.' He showed Howard Horse and Hattie into his office which was decorated in gold, and furnished with the finest Italian furniture. Sparkling pink chandeliers hung from the centre of the ceiling.

"Wine? Orrrrrrrrrrr would you like to trrrrrrrrrrrrry zome cheeseeeee? We have the fiiiiinnnnnest, you know."

Vincent was an Italian mouse who not only rolled his R's but had an annoying habit of speaking very slowly.

Howard Horse replied, "nah, we're good, gaffer."

"So...What brrrrrrrings you herrrrrrrre?" Vincent enquired.

"Well Vinnie, you know I'm in the music biness?"

"Yes. I've been made awarrrrreeeee."

"I got an offer you can't refuse." Howard Horse took out a business card from his pocket and placed it on the desk. Vincent picked it up and read aloud, "Ze Mice Boys?"

"These geezers are part of my lot, my entertainment agency, *Take a Butchers.* I 'ave worked my fingers to the bone to get 'em mainstream radio play. You know the track, *More Cheese Please, Give Me More Cheese?* That's us, mate! We've got a platinum disc displayed in our entertainers museum at our gaff now. We like to call it, the Galaxy Gallery," Howard said proudly.

Howard Horse moved in closer to face Vincent, "what about The Mice Boys 'aving a stint here, Vinnie?"

Vincent raised an eyebrow, "and what do you want in rrrrrrrrrrrrrrretrrrrrrrn?"

Howard Horse replied with a smug smile as he leaned back, "cheese of course!"

"Cheese?" Vincent sounded surprised.

"Yeah, I 'eard you got the finest in town...what do ya say?"

"Do they dance, my frrrrrrriend?" Vincent smirked.

"Are you having a bubble? You'll get the full monty, Vinnie."

Vincent reached out to shake Howard's hoof. They both whispered some numbers to each other to agree a cheese amount. After a few seconds they nodded and smiled at each other.

"Ciao!" Vincent said.

Howard winked, "pleasure doing biness wit ya Vin."

"What was all that about?" Hattie said as she and Howard left Vincent's office.

"That my treacle, is 'ow you do biness. My job is to secure work for Galaxy Garden animals by putting on entertainment, for which we get paid with food. The swanky cheese and wine shops really like The Mice Boys, 'Attie. They really pull in the sausage and mash for us. That deal you just saw, is proper cushti. Their cheese is pukka; the best Italian! Lovely jubbly for ya New Delhi."

11

The Unexpected Canister

"Are you 'avin a cream cracker Villie?"

Silence.

"Right, we're coming back, 'ole son. I'll get 'er back sharpish!" Howard Horse pressed the 'end call' button on his Bluetooth and immediately turned and trotted in the opposite direction.

" 'Attie, we're gonna 'ave to go back to the Galaxy Garden I'm afraid. Villie, you know, Neville Natterjack - the toad lad? He just called. Gartoid Manderboy is on the loose."

"I'm not going!" Hattie said sternly.

"Listen treacle, I promise I'll take you to Mia's another day, but we've *gotta* go. You're the 'alo girl, ent ya?"

"I'm going to see Mia!" Hattie said sharply. Howard brought his trotters to a stop and said, "well, doh ray mi! *I* fought you we're gonna 'elp us with this 'alo biness?"

Hattie slid down Howard's back and stood with her arms folded.

"I don't even know what to do with the halo anyway," she protested.

"The Galaxiers will 'elp ya 'Attie, you know that treacle. But listen, yeah, I can't 'ang about 'ere, me friends need me. You coming or not?"

"No, I'm not coming!" Hattie replied.

Howard Horse sighed and pointed with his hoof towards the sky, "you see those dark clouds? That means the 'alo is coming and it's gonna drop straight into the Galaxy Garden any minute now. The Galaxiers *need ya 'Attie!*"

The look on Hattie's face told Howard he should give up trying.

" 'Ave it *your* way, treacle. Ya can't bring a muzzle to water, can ya!"

Howard galloped away leaving Hattie stranded. Almost immediately, regretting her decision, a tear rolled down her cheek. She wiped it away telling herself that the Galaxiers would understand and forgive her. After all, they had each other, unlike her!

She walked the rest of the way, until she reached Mia's house. She knocked lightly on the front door.

Auntie June appeared. She looked over Hattie's head to see if anyone had come with her.

"Hattie, where's your mam?"

"Ummmm..."

"Have you come ere by yourself? Lord have mercy! Didn't we tell you...? That's it - inside!"

No sooner was Hattie bungled into the flat by Auntie June, than Mia rushed into the hallway, literally wrestling Hattie for a hug. They hugged each other, neither of them wanting to let go. Their smiles were as wide as a never-ending rainbow. It was lovely to be reunited with her bestie.

"Hattie...you do know I'm calling your mother, don't ya?" Auntie June interrupted.

Hattie lowered her chin and stuck out her bottom lip ready to burst into tears. Feeling sorry for both girls, Auntie June said in an unusually cheery voice,

"In the meantime, it's smoodie night. You're well in luck. I'll tell ya what we've got,

Apple, onion and chips smoodie
Banana, cooked liver and mushrooms smoodie
Black pudding lumps, gherkins and burnt turkey smoodie
Cut up toenails, vinegar and spinach smoodie

Blueberries, mouldy cheese and 100% dark chocolate smoodie
Shredded pig intestine and melon smoodie

So, which flavour would you like?"

"Can I have melon and banana smoothie instead, please, Auntie June?"

Auntie June rolled her eyes, " 'Attie, you always choose some revolting combination don't you? As long as you keep your paws off my Fire-cracking, HotHot, Chilli Sizzle, Razzmatazz, Sass Crisps" she winked.

"Gwan, you two. Out!"

Hattie and Mia skipped off, arm in arm to Mia's room. They giggled as they flung themselves, shoulder first onto Mia's bed. They laid on their stomachs with their arms folded underneath their chest facing each other.

"I've got a big, BIG secret!" Hattie announced gleefully.

"Go on...tell me." Mia said eagerly. "What is it?"

TAP TAP. TING TING TING. TAP.

The girls stared at each other momentarily before looking towards the sound coming from Mia's bedroom window. A bird was perched on the windowsill.

"Ignore it; it'll go away," Mia said. Hattie didn't reply but just kept staring at the bird. She walked over to the window slowly. The first thing she noticed was the bird's crimson nails.

"Um Mia...could you get my smoothie from Auntie June? I'm really thirsty."

"Yeah ok, but leave that bird alone, it will probably try to eat ya fingers, hehehehe."

"Yeah, I will," Hattie's voice trailed off. The minute Mia left, Hattie opened the window.

"Peggy Pigeon! What are you doi—?"

"YOU Hattie," Peggy Pigeon interrupted, "were meant to be at the Galaxy Garden hours ago! You need to get back NOW. We need you."

"I'm not coming back, Peggy. I'm staying here."

"Please come now, Hattie. The halo is waiting."

"No, Peggy, I can't. I can't just leave my best friend; I just got here—"

"Oh, Hattie," Peggy said in a more measured tone, "you haven't told anyone about the Galaxy Garden, have you? You can't Hattie; you can't."

"No, I haven't. I haven't," Hattie replied.

Peggy sighed with relief.

"Good. Good. Because you know what would happen, don't you?" Hattie did not reply.

"Now. Do you remember the name of our archenemy?"

Hattie nodded. "Gartoid Manderblythen?"

"Yes, well, he's unfortunately found the Galaxy Garden. We knew it would only be a matter of time. We've followed his every move at *Fortuna Sinkatron;* that's his science lab dear, but for some reason, the Brainless Blue Tits didn't see him leave today and it's caused us quite some trouble. You see Hattie, the halo belongs to Gartoid. The Mice Boys and their posse thought it would be some sort of revenge to steal it when they were forced out of Buckingham Palace but Gartoid has been on our coattails looking for the halo ever since. We always knew he was getting closer. Now, he knows where we live and he's committed the most horrible crime against the Galaxiers. The halo has appeared so you can keep us safe, but if you don't come *now*, I don't know what will happen." Peggy lowered her head and a tear fell from her eye.

"But, I, I'm...with my friend now. I'll be back later." Hattie said reassuringly. She tried to shoo Peggy away, as she could hear Mia's footsteps fast approaching.

"Got it Hattie. Here's your smoothie. My Auntie said you're staying here tonight. Your mum will get you at 7.30 tomorrow morning to go to school. You can borrow some of my clothes but I think you're in *big* trouble."

Hattie closed the window abruptly and turned to face Mia, trying to look as if she'd not just been speaking to a pigeon.

"It's not fair! Why do I have to move house? It feels just like when my parents split up and I had to leave my dad in Jamaica. It was so quick. I hardly see him at all now." She took the frothy smoothie from Mia; staring into it, she asked,

"Is my mum *really* mad?"

"Yep. Said she'll talk to you tomorrow." Mia replied, staring out of the window.

"That pigeon is flying really fast. Probably running late for its dinner hehehehehe."

Nervously, Hattie laughed and said, "yeah, probably."

12

Auntie June's kitchen was just like Hattie remembered it - long and narrow with stacks and stacks of HotHot, Chilli Sizzle, Razzmatazz Sass boxes of crisps. There were jars of homemade big toe and chocolate biscuits on a shelf, packs of water bottles and cartons of juice stacked on the floor. A charred Dutch pot sat on the stove and Auntie June's beloved Tupperware cupboard had plastic bags stuffed into each other, bursting out the side of the cupboard. Auntie June re-used everything - so embarrassing!

Propped up against Auntie June's refrigerator, were two worn out brooms, a mop and bucket and a dusty old hoover. Her vegetable basket was crammed between her cooker and the kitchen door, so the door wouldn't fully open.

Auntie June was busy packing food into Tupperware as she spoke, sounding louder than usual,

"You're running late missus. It's twenty-past seven. You've not even eaten yet. Ya mam will be 'ere at 7.30, you'll 'ave to take your breakfast with you, yeah?"

Hattie smiled and nodded.

"Auntie June?"

"Yes Attie." Sometimes she dropped the 'H' in Hattie.

"Can I have some of this lettuce?"

"At this time of the morning? Ok, if that's what you want."

"And can I have some of those tomatoes?"

"Go on then."

"And this bread and that cheese?"

"Take what you want darling. Always putting weird combinations together aren't you?" Auntie June muttered.

Cheeky mare thought Hattie. After her incredulously stinky food combinations created enough IBS and flatulence to blow up a fart factory!

Hattie rummaged through the Jenga wall of plastic bags, searching for something to pack the food in, that Auntie June gave her. She planned to share it with the Galaxiers after school.

"This is your lunch." Auntie June said, handing Hattie a large yellow margarine tub.

"You can never have too much food," she said smiling. Hattie checked the tub which had...

A packet of banana chips
Fried chicken and onion in coco bread
Dark chocolate bar with plantain flakes
A bottle of homemade carrot juice
One fried dumpling
A slice of banana pudding

7:28am, Ava sounded her car horn violently. Hattie gave Auntie June a big hug.

"Thanks Auntie June," she said.

"No problem 'Attie— Mia, aren't ya gonna say goodbye to Hattie? She's leaving now."

Mia stood in the kitchen doorway with her arms folded. She had a vexed look on her face. She was still mad at Hattie for not revealing her secret before Peggy Pigeon turned up yesterday. She also thought Hattie was showing off about her new garden.

As Hattie was unsure what to say to Mia, she left Auntie June's flat without saying goodbye to her.

"Hattie, that is the last time. Do you hear me? Do you hear me? The last time! You CANNOT, under any circumstances, just leave. When Auntie June called to tell me you were at Mia's house, I was so worried about you. What if something happened to you?"

"I just wanted to see Mia," Hattie replied with an attitude in her tone.

"You know you're grounded, don't you? Two weeks! And no pocket money."

"I've got nowhere to go anyway," Hattie mumbled under her breath.

Hattie was happy to be home after a horrible day at school which was not helped by wearing Mia's badly fitting clothes. Some girls made fun of her margarine tub at lunch. They thought it'd be fun to call her *Hattie Hattie Butter Pattie*.

Tired and frustrated, she quickly changed out of Mia's clothes into her favourite dungarees and Hatzweze trainers. She gathered the food that Auntie June had given her, ran down the stairs and yanked open the concertina door. She stepped into her garden and stopped abruptly. There were random black circular patches covering sections of the grass. She walked as quickly as she could along the centre path and approached the Galaxy Garden Rosebush HQ. Looping the plastic bag of food over her left arm, she got down on all fours.

As she was crawling through the rosebush, she found mounds of rubbish strewn along its path. There were discarded cans that she'd never seen before and random scraps of paper.

As she pushed her way through the winding stems of the rosebush, the silence was eerie. There was a pile of ants; their worker bodies tightly packed together - DEAD. She gasped! A group of ladybirds, their wings splayed as if trying to hang on to each other. Also, DEAD. Hattie continued to crawl until she reached the Galaxy Garden entrance. Except this time, the pink wall of roses no longer blocked her path. Only broken petals remained on the ground. She stopped momentarily to survey the dome. She was horrified. The Galaxy Garden had been completely destroyed! The Great Galaxy Table was in pieces. The Treehouse next to the Galaxy Tree,

GONE. The rock water feature, CRUSHED. The signs on the doors, were crossed out in mud. The bedroom doors left wide open, like they had been hurriedly abandoned. The flower borders as black as coal - DESTROYED.

Hattie ran to check the kitchen and bathrooms. NOTHING and NO ONE was there. She ran back into the dome and pulled herself up onto what was left of the Great Galaxy Table. Her feet slid as she struggled to keep her balance. She found a stable spot and sat down. Underneath the rubble of the table, were a group of cabbage worms squashed into a red pulp.

"Oh no," Hattie gasped. "This is all my fault?"

Tears ran down her cheeks and she began to cry. Had she failed the Galaxiers? Peggy had begged her to come back but she was too stubborn and selfish to listen. Through her tears, Hattie could see a white piece of paper on the ground wavering in the breeze. She slid off the Great Galaxy Table to see what it was. Although it was a struggle, she lifted a sizeable chunk of broken table leg, under which the piece of paper was trapped. Written in mud, the paper read:

'You've got something that belongs to me!'

Hattie quickly dropped the paper as if it was sizzling hot and raced back through the rosebush to head home. When she reached what used to be the Galaxy Garden entrance, she fell onto her knees, to crawl through the rosebush. Her Hatzweze trainers dragged along the ground as she pushed through the interwoven stems. She winced as the branches pricked her arms through her t-shirt.

Eventually she reached her back garden. She stood up and peered into the sky. It was cloudy. She sensed it was about to rain. She ran up the garden's main path, yanked open the concertina doors and hurried to her bedroom. She sat on her bed and reached under her pillow for a pen and her journal. Why would Gartoid vandalise such a beautiful sacred place? Hattie thought. If only she returned when Peggy had asked. Now everything and everyone was gone! Hattie straightened her diamonté cat eye glasses and started to write:

Dear Diary,

I don't know what happened today but I feel so bad. To start with, my mum is mad at me. I also haven't got any friends at school and the one friend I have, Mia, is not speaking to me because she said I was showing off, which I wasn't. Now the Galaxy Garden is gone too, and some Galaxiers are even dead.

It's all my fault, isn't it? It's me. I really don't have any friends now. It's so not fair. I just want my dad.

PS. - I wasn't showing off. I only told Mia about my new garden. It's not my fault that she doesn't have one. I really really wasn't showing off and this is all not fair. Are the Galaxiers ever coming back?

Hatz

13

Circus Bomb

Every day for two weeks, Hattie went to the Galaxy Garden hoping to find someone, but no Galaxiers were spotted. If only she could make everything right again. She missed Peggy and mischievous Missie Mouse; even the fart breath Natterjack...and Howard Horse, where did he go?

She thought that, as she WAS the halo bearer, surely, she had some power to get the Galaxiers back. In one week she:

✦ Shouted to the sky for the halo

✦ Sang to the clouds for the halo

✦ Brought toy animals and moved them around the Galaxy Garden everyday to pretend they were the Galaxiers, hoping the halo would re-appear

✦ Googled the halo

✦ Checked on the Electoral Roll for the halo...

Nothing worked and Hattie didn't know what else to do. Mia still wasn't talking to her and the best friend auditions was a disaster. The only thing she had to look forward to was her annual circus trip. She usually went with Mia, but this year it would just be her and her mum.

Hattie and her mum arrived at the giant teepee for the Crazee Circus Show on a Saturday afternoon. They had the best view of the stage from their front row seats. Hattie gave her mum a bear hug to thank her for this treat. She was so excited. She always had the best time on trips with her mum, as it brought back memories of her life in the Caribbean.

She remembered going to the carnival with her parents in Jamaica - when they were together that is. She would slurp snow cones with multi-coloured sticky syrup on top and devour packets of spicy roasted peanuts wrapped in grey paper parcels. The paper parcels were shaped like a pencil with the top torn open, which made it easier for her to pick out the nuts. After finishing her own, she would share the last of her dad's fried peppered shrimps. Then, he would hoist her onto his shoulders and follow the parade of carnival performers on float trucks to the sea front. They danced to the *jump-up jump-up* steel pan music until she was half asleep. She remembered her parents swinging their hips to the calypso music as they laughed and hugged each other. The weather was always scorching hot and everyone came; the neighbours, the mayor, and even police officers who were still wearing their gun belts. The smell of fried dumpling, ackee and salt fish, burnt sweetcorn and roast breadfruit would linger in the air for days after the carnival was over. She wished some day she could go back.

Although the circus was nothing like those memories, Hattie was excited as the lights dimmed in the teepee, signalling the opening act. Hattie got her tablet ready to take photos of the show.

From the highest trapeze, a woman in an orange glitter leotard and shiny ballet shoes swung overhead throwing glitter over the audience. Everyone cheered and screamed with excitement as some tried to catch the glitter. The Crazee Circus Show had now begun.

After half an hour, there was a fifteen-minute intermission. Hattie went to the toilet but had to queue as some of the toilets were out of order. On her way back, she wandered into the main stadium as she could hear chatter and laughter. Some children had escaped from their parents to sit and stare at the magic tricks being performed by a lanky clown. There were gasps of excitement and giggling as mime acts and funambulists showed off their daring skills. Hattie walked past a few merchandise stalls, burger stands and pop-up shops selling popcorn, candy and souvenirs. She noticed that between the candy stand and the souvenirs pop-up shop, there was a bright pink and yellow door marked, 'Private - The Circus Office.' It was ajar.

Standing inside the Office, was a man dressed in green combat trousers, a long-sleeve white shirt and a brown safari hat, with the Crazee Circus Show logo on the front. He was facing what looked like a large fish tank with a red rim, positioned on a wooden table. He stared at it intently. Hattie wasn't being nosy or anything, but she noticed the man was talking to the fish tank. She moved a bit closer, stopped and listened.

"The girl is no good fella; she's not up for the crack." A deep voice said.

"So, you really going ahead with this gaffer?"

"I'm trusted by my peers. There's no reason for this not to work." The deep voice continued.

"If that's the case, tell us where to find our Blue-faced Leicesters? You've known for months now. What's the hold-up?"

"You need to watch your mouth, bwoy; I'm calling the shots here. Give me what I want, and you'll get the exchange, yuh understand."

"Do you even know where they are?" Asked the man with the circus logo hat.

"I told you - you fool, button it! A real man keeps his word; yuh know that."

Hattie listened intently. She moved a bit closer as they continued talking.

"Have you got pictures of them, so we know everything is as it should be?" A bunch of photos landed on the ground.

"Here, tek dem and tek my photos too. How long will it take to get it done?"

"Well, we'll finish off your application, and we should get it back in about eight weeks. Then we'll book your flight."

"Good, good. I'm looking forward to teking what I've worked for. You'll get what I've promised. Yes, we'll talk again soon."

The man turned to leave the Office. Hattie ducked to avoid his gaze and pretended to continue walking. She hurried back to her seat, just in time for the second half of the circus show.

After the circus show ended, Hattie and a group of other children headed to the stage, as they all had meet and greet tickets. This was her final treat of the day.

Hattie was first in line. All the children stood neatly in line as if they were about to meet the Queen. As the circus performers arrived, each child took selfies with them. While the performers walked down the line to meet the other children, Hattie noticed the man this time with the circus logo on the back of his cap appear backstage. She watched as he lifted a blanket from what looked like that fish tank again. Though she couldn't make out what was in it, she could see an inflatable pool to his left, which had steam rising out of it. The man walked over to the sand covered stage and gathered clumps of dirt, which he threw into a bucket. He returned to the inflatable pool and carefully deposited the sand around its edges. He repeated this a couple of times, before leaving.

Shortly after, another man dressed in a fluorescent green suit and dark green tie appeared backstage. He wore sheer white gloves and carried a green suitcase. He placed the suitcase on a table and opened it carefully. Hattie stood on tip toes, trying to make out what was in the suitcase, but she couldn't. Whatever it was, it looked brown and was shaped like stones. He removed them from the suitcase and placed them on the sand on the edges of the inflatable pool. When he finished, he stood with his back straight, holding a golden bell labelled, 'NB' between his index finger and thumb. A few moments later, he rang the bell and the backstage lights dimmed.

As the performers continued down the meet and greet line, Hattie noticed the man with the circus logo cap re-appear backstage. This time, he was carrying the fish tank with the red rim. He poured the contents into the inflatable pool. Then, he walked over to a line of light switches on the wall and flicked them on. Disco lights began to flash backstage and music started to play lightly in the background. A line of people wearing swimwear then filed in. They all leant forward and nodded before they stepped into the pool. It looked like they were paying homage to someone. Hattie tried desperately to see who, or what it was, but she left without a glimpse.

Later that night, Hattie was in bed going through her photos from the circus trip on her tablet. The pictures she had with the main trapeze artist were cute. Hopefully, once they were talking again, she would show these to Mia. Towards the end of the photo reel, something caught her eye in one of the pictures!

"OMG!" she screamed as silently as she could, trying not to wake her mum. Someone had photo bombed her picture! She knew she recognised that voice!

It was. It really was! The Galaxy Garden *had* a traitor!

14

Natter-prat Trap

"Howard Horse is running late, so I've been asked to attend a meeting for him. Well, it's some dog who's been separated from their best friend. They need the Galaxy Garden to reunite them. I'm waiting for her now...it's all a bit dilly if you ask me."

Hattie sat nervously in the local supermarket café, a few seats behind Neville Natterjack Toad. He continued his phone conversation seemingly oblivious to her.

"Yes, I'll get it all sorted, Winston. I'll be on my way after this meeting, after she gets here," he tutted.

Hattie was wearing her denim dungarees, a Golden Retriever dog mask and faux dog paws she'd bought from the costume section in the supermarket. She shivered at the slimy baritone of Neville. He gave her the creeps. Big time creeps! She was puzzled. Why was he here? After all, she had called Howard Horse to meet her, NOT Neville. Well, actually, it was really to meet Hina the dog, the new alias she had created for herself. Well, Hattie felt that the Galaxiers wouldn't talk to her now as she had abandoned them when the Galaxy Garden was destroyed. She thought the best way to expose Natterprat was to pretend that she was a dog. Only then could she find the new Galaxy Garden and speak to Peggy Pigeon - if Peggy would speak to her that is - but she couldn't do that now! Not with Neville here! She disappeared into her seat like quicksand, to ponder her next move:

"I'm not waiting any longer." Neville said loudly after 'Hina' didn't show up. He hopped out of his seat and headed towards the door. In a split second, Hattie discarded her dog costume and followed him.

Neville hopped along the streets of Wembley in his light brown suit jacket using his cane to help him along. Hattie followed him from a safe distance for about fifteen minutes, ducking in and out of shop doorways to make sure he didn't see her. Then, he stopped and entered *Top Toads*, a suit and tie shop for stylish toads.

He spent about fifteen minutes in *Top Toads* before heading out and walking straight into *Spa Toads*, a sand and spa parlour on Beautilicious Lane. When he emerged, his skin was ten shades darker than when he went in. He strutted down the street like the cat that got the Crème Fraiche!

About ten hops down Beautilicious Lane, he stopped and checked over his shoulder before slipping down an alleyway. On the left side of the alleyway, there were a row of overgrown willow trees and on the right side, fences lined the back gardens of houses. Neville knocked lightly on a scraggy wooden gate with his cane. Hattie crouched near a hedge and watched him.

The man with the hat that Hattie remembered seeing at the circus, opened the gate. He stooped to Neville's height. Neville handed him a brown paper bag and walked away, closing the gate behind him. Neville left without any words being exchanged between them. Hattie observed Neville intently through a gap in the hedge as he continued to hop further down the alleyway. She followed him cautiously, but her breathing was shorter as she became tired from the heat of the midday sun. Neville then ducked out of the alleyway and disappeared.

Hattie hurried to where she saw him last, jumping over mud dips along the way. She climbed up a nearby sycamore tree to look for him. As she steadied herself, she barely glimpsed his slimy feet as he hopped into a garden. Then, he disappeared again.

She swung her legs over either side of a sturdy branch to get a better view. Craning her neck, she peered into the back gardens. Some had enlarged shrubbery and poplar trees, making it difficult for her to see where he'd gone, but something caught her eye. Through the gaps in the trees of one garden, she could see two swimming pools next to each other. One was shaped like someone in a squat position and the other was shaped like a dumbbell. Sand heaps with various sized stones and rocks, surrounded both pools. This garden was beautifully landscaped with shrubs and border flowers evenly spaced out along the hedges.

In front of the trees, Hattie vaguely saw a dome-shaped rose bush but had to squint to see clearly, as some over-crossed stems obscured her view. She could see faint flashing lights and was almost sure she heard music. To get a better view, she shuffled forward to the end of the branch and leaned over. Hattie stretched as far as she could to look between the interwoven stems. She glimpsed the end of a table, covered with culinary delights and noticed a tree next to it, which had a Treehouse on the right hand side. She'd seen a tree like this before. And, she'd definitely experienced a spread like that before! OMG! It couldn't be! She clasped her hands over her mouth in disbelief. After all her efforts of searching - this was it? She felt relieved and nervous at ' the same time.

"Neville Natterjack has actually walked into a Mice Banquet!" She mouthed the words to herself and watched as the roof of the rose bush transformed itself into a stage. The Mice Boys, wearing red velvet tuxedos were in full action, crooning the crowd of animals that surrounded the dome. After they'd finished and taken a bow, the Afro Bees ran onto the stage. They were dressed in yellow and black striped tracksuits with 'GG Afro Bees' imprinted on the back. They folded their arms across their chests in that and what? pose.

"Not sure why they bothered." Hattie murmured, "aren't they yellow and black anyway?"

The Bees had different shaped afro hairstyles. One had a round fro (like the Jackson Five in their day), another, had the high-top fade with blonde highlights on top (like the Fresh Prince). The next bee had small plaits going in all directions. The last bee, behind the DJ decks, had canerow plaits with zig-zag partings (like a young Usher). They looked ready to perform, wearing grills, gold chains and blacked-out sunglasses. They grabbed their mics and started rapping:

Afro Bees
Back in town
Switching it up to that hip hop sound
The beat is sick
Hear da bass drum kick
Let's rock out br br break dancin'

Honey so good
Sticky on top
Never get my wings caught in the trap
For that good good
Flowers and honey
Antennas see what smells like money

We're the Afro Bees! Bees Bees
Been Overseas, seas, seas
Now we got the key, key key
To the Galaxy, see, see
We're the Afro Bees, bees, bees
Honey is the fee, fee fee
We got the key, key, key

To the Galaxy see, see
Deadly
Rolling 4 deep
Never miss a show
Never miss a beat
Everyone loves our honey so sweet

We're famous
At Vinnie's Cheese Bites
We work for cheese and honey fries
So super
You know how we do
Afro Bees limousine
Rolling through!

They repeated the chorus, then they started waving their arms from side to side, willing the audience to join in. They repeated,

HEY, HO, HEY HO HEY, HO, HEY...

The Galaxiers knew all the lyrics and sang along. Even Hattie, got lost in the moment. She clapped and practised her robot moves as she sat in the tree. Howard

Horse and Missie Mouse skanked at the front of the stage while Peggy Pigeon tapped her claws. They were all having so much fun. Then, the Afro Bees dropped the mic simultaneously and exited the stage. There was a roar of applause.

This must be the new Galaxy Garden, Hattie thought. WITHOUT HER!

She slumped back onto the tree, feeling dejected. She had to find a way of getting into the new Galaxy Garden, so she could speak to Peggy Pigeon. But how?

15

Squatpump Masters

Hattie watched the entire Mice Banquet. She was sad that the Galaxiers had found a new home and moved on without her. She was about to climb down the tree to go home when she noticed six low-flying seagulls.

They swooped towards the Mice Banquet, crashing into each other as they landed on the back fence. Two almost fell, one stumbled, another slipped, and the remaining two tried to help the others get back on their feet. Once steady, they collectively squawked and huddled together, whispering. They repeatedly stopped and stared into the Galaxy Garden.

After a few minutes, they put their beaks together, squawked six times as if they were about to embark on a team sport. They lined up and surveyed the Garden, evenly spacing themselves out so that they covered the entire length of the fence. The music continued to play, and the light hum of voices could still be heard.

At first, Hattie thought the seagulls were security guards for the animals - like the Galaxy Garden Brummie chickens; but when they raised their wings and poised their toes, she knew that the Galaxiers were in trouble.

Within seconds, they were off! They swooped into the Garden with vigour and speed, swiping at sandwiches, gulping drinks, taking crisps, ham and the precious cheese. You name it; they took all of it. They stored their ill-gotten bounty between some tree branches. Swooping back and forth from the Garden to the conifer trees, they made several trips until there was almost no food left! The Mice Banquet was now a mice racket.

Loud screams, moos, baas, buzzing, fluttering, neighing, and sounds of feet stomping and running could be heard. Hattie put her hand over her ears as the pandemonium ensued. The seagulls snapped at any animal that tried to stop them.

"Greedy beggars," Hattie said aloud.

As Hattie looked up, she noticed that the sky was slowly turning from dusk blue to aubergine. Thunder struck and lightning flashed. In its magnificent glory, the golden halo appeared in the distance. It soared from the sky with vigour and purpose and its flashing multi-coloured gems glimmered like stars at night. Hattie was delighted. The halo was on its way, coming to save the Galaxiers and *she* was the halo bearer. This was the moment she'd been waiting for, to show the Galaxiers that she was sorry for turning them away.

She clambered down the tree as quickly as she could and ran towards the back gate. The halo hovered over the Garden, even as the seagulls were still circling, to check they had stolen every scrap of food.

Hattie watched and waited impatiently as the halo started to descend. The second it was low enough, Hattie burst through the back gate and entered the garden.

She looked around frantically for the rosebush. She saw it secreted in the back corner of the garden. Hattie ran towards it, stopped at the entrance and began to crawl through. She waded through the dense undergrowth as fast as she could, scuffing her knees on the ground in the process.

At last, she was in! She had expected to find another wall of roses blocking her path, like the rosebush entrance at her house, but she soon found herself standing in the middle of the rosebush dome. It was much smaller than the one in her garden!

Hattie ran towards the luminous halo as it continued to descend. She was sure she could hear whisperings from the Galaxiers as she got closer,

"Is that Hattie?"

"What is *she* doing here?" she heard someone bellow as she zipped past.

Most Galaxiers were hiding under the table. Others were busy trying to shoo the seagulls away. Howard Horse reared up on his front hooves to fight back.

"Oi! You tea leaves! Get your barking beaks off our clobber!" Howard bellowed.

Hattie could see Missie Mouse hiding food in her mouse hole. The birds on the other hand, huddled together in the Galaxy Garden Treehouse where Peggy Pigeon blocked the doorway, so the seagulls couldn't get in.

"My goodness, watch my claws. I don't usually get my nails chipped!" Peggy yelped.

In the midst of the mayhem, the halo lingered in the air.

Watching the halo, Hattie clambered onto the table and hurried to stand under it. She wanted to show the Galaxiers that she was ready to be a part of the team again. Taking her position under the halo, she announced,

"I'm really sorry everyone and I'm really sorry to Peggy for not being a good friend. I thought something happened to you all. I was worried, but I'm glad you're all ok; I'm here to help now. Just tell me what to do, ok?" She had to ask because she hadn't actually had to use the halo in a crisis before.

"Why won't it come down?" Hattie groaned.

"Am I standing under it the right way?"

She looked up expectantly, and shuffled her body to a different position on the table.

"Come DOWN!" she bawled. The halo still hovered above, gleaming like a lighthouse, not moving from its position. But why won't it crown her as it did before?

"Who are you?" came a voice from behind. Hattie turned around quickly. Two boys approached her. One boy had a t-shirt with the word SQUAT written on the front and the other boy's t-shirt read, PUMP. When they stood side by side, it read, SQUAT-PUMP. Actually, wasn't that the shape of the pools? Hattie thought. Ok – focus!

"Who are you guys?" Hattie demanded.

Ignoring her question, they hissed in a slow drawl, "why are you trying to stand under our halo? We've just come back from our horse riding competition. Move out of the way! You don't even know how to work it, do ya?"

The boys climbed onto the table and barged past Hattie. Immediately, the halo descended, duplicating itself into two. Like angels, wings appeared on the boys' backs and they ascended gracefully into the air. The seagulls quickly made their escape bumping into each other as the luminous halo began to singe their feathers.

16

Headlights

The conjoined chicken security guards appeared unexpectedly and pulled Hattie forcibly from the table. They linked her arms and marched her away.

"Get off me!" She screamed.

"Alright, alright, stop aggin. We're only going to the Galaxy Treehouse Office; we ain't going into town, kid."

They forced Hattie to climb the Garden trellis ladder which led to the new Galaxy Garden Treehouse Office. They shoved her and shouted, "go on! 0121 and DO ONE" before heading down the ladder.

There was a rectangular table made from leaves and branches in the centre of the Office. Dr Vynegarr and Peggy Pigeon were seated at the head of the table, next to Neville the Natterjack who was sat in a small pool of water with sand on its edges. Hattie was surprised to see Missie Mouse seated opposite him in the pool, munching on chips - probably *missed* by the seagulls. Hattie sat at the opposite end of the table, looking like a deer approaching headlights at midnight.

She was not sure why Vynegarr or Natterjack had not been outside trying to quell the havoc.

The Office was stuffy with an uneasy air. Notice boards were piled in a corner in an untidy mess and boxes of unpacked belongings were carelessly discarded on the floor. The silence in the Office felt awkward. Everyone was clearly unsettled by the furore of the thieving seagulls as the last of their squawks could be heard in the distance.

"How did you find us, Hattie? How did you know we vere here?" Dr Vynegarr demanded instantly.

"I...I...." Hattie mumbled.

Missie Mouse chimed in, "you did what, Hattie? Magic? You dreamt of our exact location, did ya? Hehehehehe. *You're* not the halo bearer anymore Hattie. We've got the twins now coz you didn't wanna know. So, we're staying here, and it's better anyway, see the pools outside? You ain't got them have ya!" Missie jumped out of the pool and scuttled across the table towards Hattie.

"But did you bring any pavement chips with ya, Hattie, you know; from your local chip dealer? Did ya, did ya?"

Missie Mouse was now standing on Hattie's head, leaning forward, almost touching her own toes. Her face was upside down against Hattie's, dripping water all over Hattie's face. All Hattie could see, was Missie's wide beaming grin.

"Why are you in here, Missie? You're not a part of the Galaxy Board. Out!" Peggy Pigeon ordered.

Missie then tried to turn on her cutesy charm. She looked at Peggy and said, "I'm just checking if she brought pavement chips, Peeeeeggy? It would complement the chips I've got hereeeeee...and if...."

Dr Vynegarr interrupted, "fleave Missie, SIT DOWN!" Her ginger beak hit the table as she spoke.

Missie hung her head in shame. She slid down Hattie's nose, scampered across the table and jumped into the pool. She gave the Galaxy Garden board members a good soaking in the process. They all winced, trying to ignore their annoyance at Missie's intrusion.

Dr Vynegarr asked again, "I need to know how you knew vhere we vere? Did anyone follow you?"

"I....I...well..." Hattie was scared. "I....I followed Neville Nattepra...um, I mean, Natterjack. No-one knows I'm here." She nearly called Neville a prat.

"Where from, dear? Where did you follow him from?" Peggy enquired.

Hattie didn't want to tell the whole story, so she left the dog costume bit out of it. She told them she saw him coming out of Spa Toads.

"Spa Toads? Spa Toads? Neville! We're all here working hard to unpack everything, after being forced out of the last Galaxy Garden. We've put on this banquet to cheer everyone up and we've *just* been attacked by a bunch of glutinous seagulls and *you've* been sunning yourself at Spa Toads. My goodness, how much did you pay for that?" Peggy grimaced. As usual, Neville said very little.

"Well....I needed a little spruce up," Neville boasted.

"A spruce? A spruce up? I see you've spruced up your tan alright Neville...Fiddlesticks Neville! Fiddlesticks! You've got two pools here. We've bought sand, so it's just like your home, because we know you can't live without it. We've just moved in and barely unpacked a box, what more do you want? Do you want Spa Toads here now too?"

"Well, if you're up for the crack Peggy—"

Neville loved to wind Peggy up; it was super easy. Him and Peggy went back years, so, they never really fell out.

Dr Vynegarr was still annoyed and wanted answers from Hattie, "may I interrupt you both *flease...*? Hattie, vhy did you leave us? Vhy did you turn the Galaxiers away?"

"I really missed my best friend Mia, and when I got to see her, I just didn't want to leave. It's not that I wasn't going to come back. I was coming back," Hattie nodded furiously, urging them to believe her.

"So vhy are you here now?" Asked Dr Vynegarr.

"Cause I want to be your friend and help with the halo."

"Vut that is not possivle! The halo has moved on now."

Missie Mouse said in a smug tone, "yep, it has. As I said Hattie, before I was rudely interrupted by Vyngarr Vinegar, we have all moved on. We live here now, and the pavement chips are the beeswax. Ok, they're not as good as yours, but they've got good grub!

We've already had a secret Mice Banquet and not got caught, so it's definitely better than yours."

"Another un-authorised Mice Banquet?" Peggy heralded. "So you've had two parties this month. We've put this on today for your lot, and you've partied already? For goodness sake... when? When did this happen?" Peggy shouted.

"Well, actually, we've had three but don't tell the guys I told ya Pegs."

"It's Peggy!"

"Yeah, I know, that's what I said."

Peggy huffed and shook her head.

"Why can't I have the halo back?" Hattie asked.

Peggy, now agitated, replied, "because dear, you didn't want to know. The Galaxiers need someone committed to helping us, and that day, when you told me to go away, I knew we had to do something. We lost a lot of Galaxiers in that gas attack. They're gone, Hattie, they're gone! You left us with no choice. We've come here because these are the children who moved out of *your* house. Chase and Parker Squatpump. They're the halo bearers now. So, I formally request that you do not tell anyone else about the halo, because we know YOU'VE told someone."

Peggy got up and walked to the Treehouse door. She opened it and clicked her claws, "Hattie, it's time for you to leave. Friends are meant to be there for each other, and frankly, it appears you don't know how to be a friend."

"I do Peggy, I do!" pleaded Hattie.

"I'm afraid not. Do you know we've had to uproot everything just to save ourselves? We lived at your house for *close to* a year, now. We've had to root up plants, light fittings, everything – what was left that is! The only thing we couldn't move was our Galaxy Gallery. Let's hope it's not destroyed. We've spent so much time building it up. It contains the history of some of our most revered black entertainers and past kings and queens. It's been a labour of great effort. Anyway, Chase and Parker - the twins, they'll look after us here, you've got no need to worry and no need to come back. *They've* saved us today Hattie, not you!"

Peggy stood with the Treehouse door ajar waiting for Hattie to leave. Hattie stood up, lowered her head in shame, about to leave.

"Peggy..." she ventured, "I haven't said anything to anyone. I promise."

Hattie looked at Missie Mouse, Neville Natter-prat, and Dr Vynegarr willing them to believe her. They stared back at her without offering any reassurance. Only, Natter-prat sniggered, revealing his stalactite gleaming teeth against *that* top-up tan! Ugh!

Bronson and Bruiser, the chicken security guards, arrived at the Treehouse door to escort Hattie out. Hattie could hear them bluetoothing each other on the way up, trying to decide who should put which foot where.

Without any further words spoken, she descended the Treehouse. She knew she hadn't been a good friend but still didn't know what else to do to make it up to them. She couldn't even tell them about Neville Natter-prat, that warty old scrote bag. He sat there the whole time, Crème Fraiche dripping down his wretched face, Peggy's right hand man and confidante! She would never be able to expose him to Peggy because she would never be believed, or ever be the halo bearer again.

17

Reunification

While Hattie was being removed from the New Galaxy Garden by Bronson and Bruiser, she saw the twin boys floating in the air like angels. They flew over the Garden carrying something in their arms. Bronson and Bruiser instantly let go of Hattie and ran towards the twins.

The Galaxiers were busy clearing away the mess left by the vicious seagulls, but when they saw the Squatpump boys, all the insects, animals, tall, short, skinny and the clinically obese, abandoned what they were doing and encircled them immediately.

Peggy Pigeon flew down from the Galaxy Treehouse with Neville Natterjack on her back. She landed gracefully on the table where the Squatpump boys had laid something out. Hattie watched them from a distance.

The boys knelt, faced each other and touched heads. Peggy Pigeon then walked between them.

Hattie couldn't see what was on the table, but whatever it was, it was moving slightly. The boys' wings flapped slower and slower. When they were still, their wings dispersed into gold dust which whizzed upwards in rhythms and patterns. The sound of the gold dust dispersing was like the gentle breath of a baby.

Everyone marvelled as the gold dust assembled and formed into the halo. It ascended, higher and higher, until it disappeared. The boys stood up, carefully revealing what they had hidden. Peggy Pigeon stepped forward. There were sharp intakes of breaths. She addressed the group.

"Galaxiers. Your attention, please? The halo has brought us..."

Everyone waited, hanging onto Peggy's every breath. Her claws were crossed and her eyes bulged. No one appeared to breathe.

"Finally," Peggy shouted excitedly, "the halo has returned the Bluefaced Leicesters' daughter!"

"AAAAAAAAAAAHHHHHHHHHHH!!!!!!!!!!!"

No sooner had the announcement been made than screams and shouts echoed throughout the Garden. The jubilation from the Galaxiers was emphatic. Any reunification, no matter how long it took, was a triumph for all. The twin boys smiled, repeatedly jumping around with joy. The Garden, was now full of celebrations and back to what it was before the seagulls attacked it. This was a moment they had all waited for - a Galaxier being reunited with their lost family member. Hattie was so happy for them. After all the hard work of searching for the Galaxiers, none of that mattered anymore. Now was a time to celebrate. The Galaxy Garden was all about this very moment.

The two Bluefaced Leicesters stepped forward. They looked at their baby daughter and then turned to the twin boys with tear filled eyes and smiled.

The Galaxiers began to chant slowly,

" S Q U A T P U M P S , SQUATPUMPS, SQUATPUMPS, SQUATPUMPS,

SQUAT-PUMPS..." The chanting got quicker and quicker until it ended in a fast-paced crescendo of adoration.

The crowd 'pumped' (no pun intended) their fists repeatedly in the air; this was a moment of glory. The Galaxiers made themselves comfortable as the Bluefaced Leicesters sat on the table with their baby daughter wrapped in their arms. In true Galaxy Garden tradition, anyone who became reunited with their family, had to tell their story. The father, Baba Blueface, spoke up.

"We were born and raised in the Leicestershire hills. Our carers were Nigerians who settled on a farm there, so that is why we have their accent. That's also where I met my beautiful wife. This little one you see here, is our only child. The farmers adored her when she was born. Oh, oh, they looked after us really well, but something changed. They soon began to come into our home, trying to catch my wife so they could take her away! Ah ah! Not my wife! IDIOTS! So, every time they came into our home, I said, 'Come here. What in the name is going on?' They would tell me to close my eyes and that it would be over quickly. So, I asked them, 'are you magicians?' They were not Paul Daniels, or that foolish boy, David Blaine. NO! I had to protect my family.

I soon overheard the farmers saying they expected more children from us. So, they made plans to crossbreed other animals with my wife. Lord have mercy! I guess they got fed up with fighting me, because two days later, they took all three of us out. After a short while, they pushed my wife and I off the tractor and kept our baby. They just kept on driving even as I shouted at the farmer, 'Boodoukweh, COME HERE.' That farmer, she is so disobedient; I will have to say a prayer for her later. We ran after them but couldn't catch up. Aaah! My wife couldn't feed our baby with her own milk. My Jesus!

After a few weeks, we were soon transported from the farm to somewhere in London, where they left us. We heard the new farmers say that they were taking us somewhere new to supply the shops with the finest wool. That's when I cried out, 'The blood of Jesus!' Our wool is popular with the humans, you see. A London shop owner bought us and put us in her garden. Can you believe it? I kept crying out; Jesus have mercy. She kept us as pets just so she could put clothes in her shop. She named her shop, 'I Shaved Wool for These Cardigans.' Very stupid and silly girl! Ah Ah!

Any day soon, all our hair would be gone. We'd be butt naked. Naked! Jesus will be shaking his head, ah ah, what in the name of God is going on here? Really? I have a beauty spot on my backside that only my wife knows about; now the whole street was going to see it. Ah Ah!

Anyway, day after day, we noticed a pigeon flying over our garden. I called out to her one day, and she asked why we as sheep, were being kept as pets. She told us about the Galaxy Garden and how it could help us find our daughter. It was only 20 doors down from our home. Within an hour, she called Howard Horse and all the dirty mice....erm...erm... I mean, the rather helpful, yes, very helpful vermin friends. They broke down the back gate and freed us. Ah! Now look at us now, eh? We have our baby daughter back. Ah! Isn't He a good God! Thank you, Peggy. Thank you, Squat-de-pumps. Thank you, Galaxiers. May God Bless you."

The Galaxiers cheered, and the music was turned on. They celebrated into the summer's evening with the remains of the food Missie Mouse had stored away during the seagull attack.

While Hattie was touched by Baba Blueface's story, she could see too, that the Galaxiers no longer needed her as they now had those annoying Squatpump twins. So, she slipped silently out of the Galaxy Garden and headed home.

18

MiDDay Smarts

Hattie still hadn't made up with Mia, even though it was the last week of the summer holidays. As she didn't have any friends to spend the holidays with, her mum sent her to the local community play scheme. She didn't think she would, but she found she missed the annoying Missie Mouse *and* Howard Horse; she missed him calling her 'treacle.' Those Squatpump twins had ousted her as the halo bearer and Peggy didn't even want to know her. If only she knew that Natterprat was up to no good!

Preoccupied with finding a way of warning Peggy Pigeon about the threat to the Galaxy Garden, Hattie let her mind and pencil wander as she doodled away in her journal, maybe she could:

- Host a Smart Pigeon Contest (Peggy is knowledgeable and is likely to attend)

- Write to Peggy Pigeon (that probably wouldn't work, as Neville opened all the post)

- Host a Mice Banquet and invite Peggy!

She doodled and crossed out several ideas before she made her final decision. A week later, she put her plans in motion.

Two finalists remained in the Smart Pigeon Contest. First was Booker. He was dressed in a pink striped suit, a light pink shirt and a red diamanté tie. He wore eight blue well polished brogues; one for each pigeon claw. He looked very sharp indeed. The second finalist, Man Like Dlux, had four gold sliders on each claw, secured by velcro straps. He wore gold socks with 'DLUX' imprinted on the sides and his bare chest glistened from a gold chain hung around his neck. The arms of his sunglasses were inscribed with the letter 'D' in gold. He looked like a very cool rap star!

Booker and Man Like Dlux, the two finalists, lined up on the podium in the corner of Hattie's back garden, ready for the contest to start. Hattie asked her first question,

"Do you ever get neck cramp?"

Booker replied, "nah, I tend to keep in shape. I look after my temple," he said stroking his chest with his wing.

"Man Like Dlux?" Hattie asked.

"Well yeah, I need to see who I'm pooping on hahahahaha."

"What? What do you mean bruv? Isn't that casting judgement on others? You can't do that!" Booker said.

"Naaahhhh bruv, it's casting *poop* bruv. Listen yeah, if you just walked past me with kebab meat and chips and you IGNORE ME bruv, that's peak! I'm a pigeon out here on the road, fam. So, if I see you for the second time and I'm sittin' high enough to dash my poop. Don't chat to me bruv! It's going to land, yeah. You already know I'm the Pigeon Papi out here!" Man Like Dlux boasted.

"Guys, no conferring please," Hattie pleaded.

"Here's question 2. I've heard pigeons have precise vision. Can you answer how that's possible with eyes stuck to the sides of your head? Give me your smartest answer."

Booker replied, with a wicked grin, "I see ALL I need to see. You get me?"

Man Like Dlux interrupted, "I've had eye surgery blood. My eyes are at the front now."

"Yeah?" Asked Booker.

Man Like Dlux smiled a shiny white smile. He took off his glasses to show off his new look. Booker turned to face him and burst out laughing.

"Wow! Are you alright Dlux? Hahaha. Are you alright bruv? Sounds like you're truly living a life of suppressed rage and denial bruv. Hahahaha—"

"Vio! Straight violation! You know I'm a high-quality brother, fam. 100% vegan bruv. Don't try to play me!"

Booker replied, "more like 100% velcro don, with those sliders!"

Hattie was confused. "Ssshhh! Why are you arguing? Back to the questions guys."

Hattie asked her next question, "is there a pigeon version of Come Dine with Me?"

"Yeah. I'm coming to yours later Hattie, to come dine wid you, trust me. Thanks for the invite." Booker said excitedly, the prospect of free food being his main motivation.

"Don't do that, Booker!"

"What Dlux?"

"She didn't invite you bro!" Dlux said annoyed.

"Is dat your answer, fam? Dlux, is that your answer
to Hattie's question?" Booker demanded.

Dlux laughed, "oh my God! Hahaha Really, blood?"

"Dlux, why you blocking for? You know she's got some fried fish and onions in her yard fam. What's wrong wid you man? Man's got needs, you get me?"

"Don't watch him Hattie. He's so cheap! Anyway, true say I'm da number one seed out ere, most pigeons just come dine with me, the Dlux fam. It's on me. *Ya get me?!"*

"Bro, you didn't understand the question." Booker said indignantly.

"*I* didn't understand the question bruv? Mr invite myself to girl's yard for two two onions. Have you always been this cheap Booker?"

"Guys?" Hattie tried to interrupt.

She repeated the question, "is there a pigeon version of Come Dine With Me?"

They both ignored her and continued the banter. Some smart pigeon contest this was! Hattie thought.

Booker replied sharply to Dlux, "listen yeah, my lawyer said I don't have to answer that question."

"What lawyer! You ain't got no lawyer bro. You own Acid and Poop Solicitors. What you talking about bruv?"

"What? You think I didn't get advice before I came here, fam?" Booker questioned.

"Are you fo real?" Dlux asked. "You're here to win CRUSTY BREAD fam! I don't know what's wrong with this guy you know." Dlux said shaking his head.

"C'mon Guys!" Hattie pleaded again. They still ignored her.

Booker clapped back. "Yo, shut up bruv! Greggs is closed ennit."

Man Like Dlux was shocked, "Greggs?! Oh my God...man's acting like he ain't got bread. He's got P you know Hattie. He's rich! I'm just here to win this Golden Love Bread for my wife. Next question, next question."

Booker couldn't wait to correct Dlux. In a patronising tone, he said, "and for the record, it's Aceed and Poupe Solicitors. You need to get it right; I represent *you* Dlux. You're my artist. Get it right, Aceed and Poupe! Capiche?"

"Bruv? Don't capiche me! It's Acid and Poop, yeah! Acid and Poop! I said what I said bruv."

Booker rolled his eyes.

"Ok. Finally." Hattie sighed as they both stopped yakking. Neither of them had really answered what she asked.

"This is your last question. Give me your smartest answer, ok? Deep pan or thin crust?"

Booker immediately answered, "definitely deep pan. Pizza Hut is locked off! So we've only got cheap pizza shops still. The standard is slipping man. It's a struggle out here."

"Yo," Dlux ventured, "...man only eats gluten free round here you know."

"Don't do that," Booker replied sharply. "Stop lying bruv."

"I told you, I'm 100% vegan man! I'm plant-based Dlux. Me and my wife eat different now."

Booker enquired, "really? I'm sure you just said a couple questions ago that you eat food out on road. Are you telling me, allllllllll of that is gluten free?"

"Is that what I said though?"

Booker smirked, "I'm just asking you..."

Man Like Dlux *cut* his eye and shouted, "move man!"

"What are you lying for?" Booker laughed. "Hattie don't know your wife. It's ok, brother - let it out man! Hahahaha."

"Yo, yo, yo. Booker? That's a vio! You know that ennit? What you just said, it's a violation. Hahaha."

Booker replied, "I know!" They both laughed. Hattie was befuddled. From the way they spoke, clearly, they knew each other. She was so lost in their incessant back and forth that she ended up sharing the Golden Love Bread prize between them. Man Like Dlux flew away with his half.

"Later yeah." He bellowed midair, as his sliders fell into the neighbour's garden.

Booker stayed behind. He turned to speak to Hattie and suddenly became serious. He asked,

"Where did you get this bread from?"

"I found it in my garden," Hattie replied.

"Ok cool, cool, cool, cool—" he paused, then started pacing. "It's just that, this type of bread yeah, is usually bought with Pigeon Paper. It's our currency still.

I was just wondering how it got into *your* hands Hattie, you get me?"

It looked like normal crusty bread to Hattie, "erm, I found it in my garden when I moved here so—"

"Ok, cool, cool, cool," Booker smiled suspiciously and handed his business card to Hattie.

"Take this, yeah," Booker said. "That's for you, yeah - and about that piece of fried fish—"

"There's no fish!" Hattie interjected.

"But I can smell the ting from ere sis," Booker insisted. He was always greedy for food. Whatever he could do to get free food, he would try.

"There's no fish Booker. Fly on! You've got your bread. FLY ON."

"That's exactly what I'm saying, your fish and my bread it's a match made for—"

"*Me* sey *gwan!*" Hattie shouted in her best patois, frustrated at Booker's persistence.

As Booker flew away, Hattie studied his business card. It read:

Aceed and Poupe Solicitors

No win no fee accident claims solicitors

We deal with claims for acid damage to:-

☑ cars,

☑ listed buildings

☑ posh frocks and suits

caused by pigeon poop

We also manage hip-hop artist: Man Like Dlux.

Hattie was disappointed that after all her efforts to get Peggy's attention, Peggy hadn't turned up to her Smart Pigeon Contest. She realised that *she* was no closer to warning Peggy Pigeon about Neville the Natterprat.

19
TAAK UP!

As Hattie was tidying away the contest banners, she thought she heard a voice. She threw the bin liner aside and hurried towards the rose bush at the back of her garden.

She clambered over what used to be the wall of roses and fell onto all fours ready to fight her way through the thick undergrowth.

Eventually she managed to burrow her way in and was standing in the abandoned dome of what used to be the Galaxy Garden. It was eerie being there without any of the Galaxiers.

The voice she heard seemed to be getting louder. So, she ran along the perimeter of the dome, trying to peer inside but could see no-one.

As she neared the back of the Galaxy Garden kitchen there was a door slightly ajar. So, she stopped outside, pushed the door open and began to crawl through it. As she was crawling through, she could smell something musty, like mouldy bread. She stayed low as she realised the voice was coming from the Galaxy Garden kitchen. When she eventually reached the kitchen door, she knelt and put her ear to the door and listened.

"Right. Right. Let me try and get this STRAIGHT." The voice spoke with a thick Caribbean accent.

"Alllll *six* a unu, me send unu out, to get back mi halo. Right? But you come tell me sey, for THREE WEEKS unu gwan fe a bashment, thief dem food, filled yuh bellies and forget about the mission that I send you fi do?"

A squawk of the seagulls sounded presumably in response.

"...and now unu, unu, unu, unu unu AND UNU, bring ME to the Galaxy Garden, fi what? Nobody is here. Er, hello? Do you see anybody in here? Nope! Nuttin!"

The seagulls squawked again.

"You avoid mi! Mi tink sey yuh dead, not filling yuh bellies, so it swell up like a hippopotamus."

Hattie craned her neck but she just couldn't see who was talking. The voice continued...

"Unu is real fool fool! Wah mek yuh so greedy? Let me remind unu, unu, unu, unu, unu AND UNU," he said raising his voice, "wha I pay yuh fe do. I want you to go and find the halo. FIND IT for me! I made it. I'm the scientist who made it and a want it back. It's my birthright. I want it back because I worked hard. FIVE YEARS! Stone by stone I put it together and these dusty likkle animals, thief IT!

The Queen just call me again yuh know. She told me that I'm the number one scientist in the world and she wants to wear my halo as a crown again. I feel so shame to tell her that I've lost it! Do you know how long that halo tek to mek? Five years! Me *naaaaah* do it! Let me tell you something, I'm not making another one. I want back *my* original halo; it doesn't matter what you have to do. I need to give the Queen back her tings, so mi want it back and mi want it back TONIGHT!"

Hattie suddenly realised who was mouthing off in what used to be the Galaxy Garden kitchen. It was *Manderblythen!* GARTOID MANDERBLYTHEN, the archenemy and his team, the Blytheners, hunting the Galaxiers to get back Gartoid's halo. Peggy Pigeon was right; Gartoid was close. It's a good job the Galaxiers were no longer at the Galaxy Garden.

The seagulls began to squawk again furiously. Something was wrong. Gartoid slowly turned. Hattie's heartbeat quickened as Manderblythen pounded his way towards her. Through a crack in the door, Hattie noticed his shoes, which were futuristic and shaped like sneakers.

"WHO YOU IS?" He

shouted as he crouched, peering through the hole in the kitchen door.

"Did you hear me? WHO ARE YOU?"

Gartoid yanked open the kitchen door. He was wearing his self-labelled white lab coat and large gold rimmed glasses. He was short and stout with caucasian looking skin. His beard was peculiar because it was brown and stubbly but his eyebrows were dark and unruly. His most striking body feature however, was his mis-shaped shoulder. It was like he'd once had a hump removed from the other shoulder which left him slightly off balance. Misery was etched on every sinew of his face.

"How do YOU know about this place?" He pointed and demanded of Hattie his voice resounding throughout the Galaxy Garden kitchen.

Silence.

"Answer mi nuh man!"

She couldn't think of what to say.

"No English?" she lied, as sweat dripped from her nose.

"Why yuh nose sweating like that? GET UP!" He shouted.

Hattie's chin began to quiver. She cowered and stayed still.

"Mi sey get up likkle girl."

Hattie slowly stood up, holding her hands firmly at her side because they were shaking so much.

"Oh you think I'm a fool?" He said nodding and grinning wickedly. "I said stand up, and you stood up, QUICKLY! Why are you lying likkle girl?"

Gartoid crouched to Hattie's level. His eyes popped out of his head with rage as he spoke.

"Likkle English girl...you better start taaking

NOW!"

20

Hallway of Mercy

Hattie eyed the seagulls closely. Somehow, she felt that she'd seen them before. Her mouth fell open and her eyes widened when she realised it was THEM!

They were the thieving reprobates that swooped unexpectedly ruining the Mice Banquet at the New Galaxy Garden. They were actually Gartoid's little minions!

Their squawking grew louder as they turned towards Gartoid for instruction. Leaving Hattie still shaking, Gartoid walked towards them.

"Mi sey simmer down. Talk to me, Blytheners. Who is she?"

They squawked frantically at Gartoid. Then, the squawking subsided as they formed a circle with Gartoid in the middle. They turned their heads quizzically, from side to side. Narrowing their fiendish eyes, they looked like they were in an intense discussion with Gartoid. Hattie tried to translate their movements but she realised something was very wrong. They were talking about her! Nervously, she looked around for an escape route. She had to get to Peggy before Gartoid and his Blytheners.

Hattie slowly stooped and shuffled her feet backwards as Gartoid and his six nincompoop Blytheners were in conversation. Their squawks silenced even further as Gartoid began to chastise them. It was then that Hattie slipped out of the kitchen unnoticed.

"I don't understand," she could hear Gartoid saying as she got further and further away.

"Shut up while I'm talking. Let me tell you lot what I don't get. Unu have 360-degree vision. That means you can see front, back and side allll at the same time. That's why I pay you. Now you're trying to tell me, you NEVER saw her sit and listen to everything that I was saying? What am I meant to do now?

I pay you with enough food, you've got everything you want, but the way unu, unu, unu, unu, unu AND UNU gwan, I may need to rename you the One Visioners, because, you are acting like you only have ONE eye. In fact, I feel a likkle disrespected. Yes, I may BBQ your backsides one day with my All-Purpose Seasoning. I haven't heard of seagull seasoning yet, but there's a possibility I could find some!"

The Blytheners, well, the One Visioners, lowered their heads and tucked their buns further into their feathers, fearing they would soon be spit roast in Gartoid's lab.

Hattie could feel her heart pounding as she hurried through the hallway towards the back entrance. The hallway was littered with black rubbish bins, like someone had been fly-tipping. She jumped over the rubbish bags as quickly as she could.

When she reached the end of the hallway, she realised that she only had two choices; make her way around the vast dome to escape, or go DOWN. She contemplated for a split second but was jolted back to her dilemma by the incessant squawking of the seagulls. She could hear their wings flapping. They must have realised she was gone.

Hattie ripped open two black plastic bin liners and emptied the contents. She quickly wrapped one around her hair and held the other in her hand. There was no time to take a deep breath as the seagulls were almost at her heels. She ducked behind the bins out of sight.

The Blytheners skidded and came to a halt. Hattie noticed that some of their feet were slightly *singed*. They surveyed their surroundings. Only the odd squawk escaped from a few beaks. There was no way she could outrun them. So she remained still and waited.

The Blytheners began to double back on themselves as they'd reached the end of the hallway. Hattie waited until they were out of sight and then hurriedly made her way down into the Galaxy Garden Rosebush sewage tunnel.

Here goes . . . **SPLASH!** She was in.

It was dark and airless, except for the small spec of light seeping through the fine mesh air pockets secreted along the wall. The ground was full of thick stodgy poo and age-old wee. She cupped some poo in her hand and stuck it into the larger air pocket where she'd crawled in. Urgh! It was super disgusting but she needed to cover her tracks. Although she knew seagulls could swim, they would certainly mess up their beautiful white feathers if they attempted to follow her in.

Hattie's feet kept getting stuck as she waded through the waist-high sewage. She could hear Gartoid yelling at the Blytheners to find her.

She ploughed forward, using the tunnel walls for support. Surely there wasn't far to go! She stopped for a second as she was out of breath. The foul smelling poo made her feel sick. Eww! She could literally taste it. She moved forwards again and could see in the distance a strong light.

"That must be the exit!" She mumbled to herself.

Before long, she was at the end of the tunnel. She reached up and pulled back a rusty bolt with all her might, and pushed the tunnel door open.

"AAAAAAHHHHHHHHHH..."

She spat out all the mess she had held in her mouth the whole time and slumped at the tunnel exit. At last! Now she would go and find Peggy Pigeon and tell her that Gartoid was on the loose and expose the Natterprat traitor! But—

"Ah, there you are," a deep voice resounded. "If you ask me, you should be going back in there. That's where YOU BELONG."

Hattie tried to look up but she couldn't see. She wiped large blobs of faeces from her eyes and shook it off her hands. Yuk! A shadow loomed over her but her eyes had not yet adjusted to the daylight. When they did, she saw the feet first.

21
Through the Triage

"Get away from me," Hattie screamed as she tried to pull herself away from his grip.

"Get in here quickly." He said as he pulled her to a nearby tree. He tapped his cane twice on the tree bark. A door opened and he shoved Hattie in. The room was set up like a lounge. There were rugs, a settee, a kitchenette and pictures of a rabbit family hung over a fire place.

"You Hattie, have been a busy girl, haven't you?"

"What do you mean?" Hattie replied.

"Well, first of all, you stink! Secondly, I'm politely reminding you to stay away from the new Galaxy Garden."

"Why?"

"If you want my advice, you should make friends with that Mia girl; otherwise, you're going to get yourself in a lot of trouble. Look at you now. You're cold, wet, you smell, and you've got no friends. No-one at school likes you and the halo is no longer yours. It's all gone to the jacks; it's over for you!"

"Leave me alone, you slime ball," Hattie screamed

"Oooooh, you've got guts, haven't you? Hahaha. Hattie Mae James, I denounce you from your halo duties, and I order you not to tell anyone about anything you have seen, and you are never to return. You, my lady, should stop creeping around; otherwise, you'll be on a plane in a couple of days. If you do tell anyone, no-one will believe you; you know that. Everyone will think you're a joke, and to be honest, hahaha, you look like one right now!"

He lowered his face closer to Hattie's and shouted, "STAY AWAY. Understand?"

He turned away from Hattie and pushed open the tree bark window. He peered outside, closed it swiftly and said, "you're lucky the halo will get rid of the Blytheners for you. The fact that I'm here, means the halo will appear whenever a Blythener and a Galaxier are in the same space because it senses a Galaxier may be in trouble. So, I'm going to leave now because the Squatpump boys, Chase and Parker, are coming to get me. On my return to the new Galaxy Garden, I will tell my peers I've seen you and YOU HATTIE won't say anything to anybody else. GOT IT?" Hattie whimpered a feeble nod. He opened the tree bark door with his cane, closed it behind him and left.

He was right. Everyone did think she was a bad friend and a joke, and no-one would believe her, not even Mia. She had nothing now, except her draws, full of crap, and it wasn't even her crap!

The next morning, Hattie and her mum had just returned home from a supermarket trip. Hattie ran to her bedroom to try on the new doggie costume she'd asked her mum to buy. She was going to use this costume as part of her new plan to show the Galaxiers that she *really* wanted to be their friend. She faced the mirror to straighten her doggie ears and repositioned her diamanté glasses. Now she was ready to put her plan into action, so she headed downstairs.

Hattie approached Ava whilst she was distracted talking on the phone. She asked if she could stay over at Shanti's house, next door, as she was having a weekend birthday party. Ava stopped momentarily and stared at

Hattie who was wearing the doggie costume, mask and dog paws.

Ava paused. "In *that* outfit, Hattie? Well ok, but make sure you bring some proper cloth—"

Hattie didn't need to hear anything else. She left the house quicker than Missie Mouse could devour a plate of chicken.

Before long, Hattie turned up at the back gate of the new Galaxy Garden. She fell onto all fours, like a dog. With her new paws, Hattie knocked the gate. The Brummie chicken security guards opened the gate. Keeping her head down, she used one paw to slide a piece of paper to them. Using their three legs, they bent down and with one of their shared arms, they opened the note which read,

My names is Hina, I lost my friend Sam. Need help to find. Help please!

The chickens bluetooth each other.

"Well. What you saying, Bruiser?"

"Yeah, he looks awright to me; let's get him in the Office."

"Wait. Don't we need to run some checks?"

"He's a chuffing dog Bronson. What kind of checks do we need? We're a secret garden, aren't we? No-one is coming in here without our say so anyway. We're good at security, ain't we?"

They looked at each other, nodded, and said in unison, "fair enough. In ya go, bab. 0121 and do one."

Hattie was shown into the newly decorated Treehouse Office. Seated around a large rectangular table was Peggy Pigeon and Neville Natterjack, the slime ball Toad lad. Before they would do anything to help Hina, they asked her to complete a risk assessment questionnaire.

Risk Assessment Questionnaire

Name: Hina the Dog

Age: 5 dog years

Birth place: London

Current Address: Homeless

Do you have any dog crime convictions?

Nope. Woof!

Have you ever hurt, scratched, or bitten a child or another animal?

Oh no! That's mean. Woof Woof!

Have you ever had or are you currently suffering from tics, lice, fleas, worms or any ongoing health condition?

OH HELL NO! I mean, woof woof woof!

Marketing: How did you hear about the Galaxy Garden?

What happened was, I, erm…I dreamt about it. Yeah, it's a miracle. Woof!

Hattie tried to answer their questions with a dog undertone so that they wouldn't notice that it was actually her. Afterwards, they asked her to step onto the Treehouse lift. It was lowered by the chicken security guards back into the Galaxy Garden. She was lead through what was now the new rosebush at the back of the Squatpump twins' garden. It looked just like the old one, except it was smaller with less plants and trees.

They led Hattie, aka Hina, to a room where Howard Horse was waiting. They handed Howard the completed risk assessment form and left.

"Ok, ok, you're a stray basically 'ent ya?" Howard Horse chuckled. "Let's see what we can do for you then, love." He fiddled with his iPad before saying, "I'm gonna ask you a few questions treacle and then, I'll pass you to the next induction, right?" Hattie, aka Hina, nodded.

Ever worked in the entertainment industry?
Woof! No but I like the circus.

Who's got the most famous cheese cafe in London?
Vinnie's Cheese Bites of course! Woof!

Do you know anything about music recording?
No, but I can learn. Woof!

Do you have a social media account?
My mum won't let me! Woof!

What's your talent?
I've danced before

Conclusion: Hina's Performance Potential - NIL

"Right fanx for that darlin', I'm gonna 'and you over to Neville Natterjack. He's going to size you up for earning potential. By the looks of this, it don't look like you can be part of me 'Take a Butcher's Entertainment Agency,' but I guess we'll see what your dancing skills are like a bit later and take it from there. Likely you'll be working in-'ouse."

"Woof," Hattie barked the deepest bark that she could summon.

She didn't really care what job she did, she just needed to get close enough to Peggy to tell her what was happening. She had overheard Gartoid saying he was still going to look for the Galaxy Garden and retrieve his halo. That meant that he could turn up at anytime, even tonight! Hattie had to get through whatever questionnaires she needed, to start her quest to speak to Peggy alone.

Before long, she was back in the Treehouse, alone with him again. The sneaky lying scrote - TRUSTED by the Galaxiers? What a joke! He couldn't be trusted as far as his hippity hoppity scaly tootsies could take him.

She sat with him and went through yet another questionnaire and the rules of the Galaxy Garden. She tried to keep her head down as much as possible, hoping that he wouldn't get suspicious. At the end of the meeting, Neville Natterjack handed Hattie a Galaxy Garden Contract. Once Hattie had paw-printed each statement, Neville Natterjack stamped her contract and agreed she could stay.

GALAXY GARDEN

CONDITIONS OF STAY

PAW PRINT TO AGREE

YOU AGREE TO SLEEP IN YOUR ASSIGNED
DOG KENNEL AND YOU AGREE TO CLEAN
YOUR POOP.

Hina, Paw Print

YOU WILL CONTRIBUTE TO THE RUNNING
OF THE GALAXY GARDEN.

Hina, Paw Print

YOU MUST KEEP THE GALAXY GARDEN A
SECRET.

Hina, Paw Print

YOU MUST FOLLOW THE GALAXY GARDEN
RULES.

Hina, Paw Print

SIGNED

PRINT Neville "King" Natterjack

Galaxy Garden Secretary and Accountant

"You must think of ways of earning money or food for your fellow Galaxiers," Neville said. Again, keeping her head down, Hattie nodded as Neville showed her to her assigned dog kennel.

Her kennel was small, barely lit and was surrounded by black metal railings. Neville Natter-prat pulled the metal door shut behind him and dropped the latch before taking leave.

Inside the kennel, was a small towel, a blanket, a dog bowl, a bowl of water and an old dog bed covered in different coloured shedded hairs.

"Yuk," Hattie muttered under her breath. At any rate, she was happy to have completed the first part of her mission; she'd made it into the new Galaxy Garden undetected. Feeling pleased with her achievement so far, she eventually found a soft warm spot on the dog bed and settled for the remainder of the evening. Tomorrow would be a big day.

22

Double Agents

The next morning, Hattie sniffed at the bowl of thick curdle-looking slime which was pushed under her nose. This was supposed to be her breakfast! It looked like dried poo on the rim of a toilet that had been scraped off and watered down into a thick gravy. It was brown and gooey. Ewww! It even smelled like a ten year old garbage bin. Hattie contemplated her options. If she ate it, she could not tell anyone. If she didn't eat it, the Galaxiers might get suspicious. She didn't want that!

Hattie lowered her head inch by inch and stuck her tongue out tentatively. Saliva started running from the corners of her mouth onto the brown thingy in the bowl. She could hardly bring herself to touch it. Great! Now, it was drizzled in spit. For goodness' sake! Hattie closed her eyes tightly and stuck out her tongue again, just to touch the tip of the dog bowl. She couldn't bear to look at it, but she crossed her fingers behind her back and dived in.

GULP

GULP

GULP

YUK! She ate it as quickly as she could until she was sure the bowl was clean. Mission accomplished! She rolled over and sprawled out on her stomach. She tried to ignore the dog slop still lodged in her teeth. She could not believe that she'd just WILLINGLY EATEN DOG FOOD. Ugh!

Tap. Tap. Tap. Hattie's kennel door opened, and she was handed paperwork which read...

GALAXY GARDEN

To: *Hina*
From *Galaxy Garden Board*
Day *Saturday*
Re: *Induction Outcome*

Dear Hina,

Your risk assessment is complete. You are the Galaxy Garden Chief Lead Dog Walker. You must organise dog trips and report to the Treehouse Office if there are any concerns.

This role starts today. Saturdays are for trips to the local Pee Pee Park. When you get back, corn beef, baked beans and salami curdle delight will be served for lunch in our very own Galaxy Galley.

Good Luck, and we hope we can reunite you with your friend Sam soon.

Kindest Regards
The Galaxy Garden Team

This was a disaster! Hattie wanted to blend in and get on with her own mission to speak to Peggy Pigeon alone. But, if she spent too much time with the natives, walking REAL dogs, they might sniff her out. Then she would be banished forever!

Before Hattie could come up with a plan to avoid her dog walking duties, the Galaxy Garden dogs were gathered outside her kennel panting, eager for their afternoon walk. She could hear them muttering that she was late. This was not a good start.

After walking the dogs, Hattie lead them back to the new Galaxy Garden. She noticed the Galaxiers surrounding Chase and Parker Squatpump who were handing out pizzas, chip butties and sandwiches. Hattie was glad it wasn't cold corned beef and sloppy salami curdle. The boys made sure everyone had something to eat, before heading back into their house. Hattie was so excited to eat real food that she almost forgot that she was meant to act like a dog. It was a task trying to eat pizza with dog paws!

As Hattie gobbled up the last piece of her cheese and pepperoni pizza, she thought she could hear raised voices in the distance, so she trotted out of the Galaxy Garden to investigate. She wandered into the Squatpump twins' patio, stooped and peered inside their conservatory.

The Squatpump twins were sitting on a sofa, hanging their heads. Hattie could only assume that it was their parents that were standing over them. They were dressed in tweed jackets, jodhpurs and bright orange jumpers thrown around their shoulders and loosely tied under their chins. Even their parents looked like twins!

From the little Hattie could hear, mommy and daddy Squatpump were shouting at the twins saying that they watched them go into the garden with bags of food, disappear, then come back to the house with nothing. Daddy Squatpump said,

"You'd better tell me what's going on, or we won't...we won't ...give you any more pocket money, or keep cleaning your pools. You'll have to clean them yourself!"

Mommy Squatpump nodded in agreement. Suddenly, the twins began to speak very quickly. Hattie couldn't make out what they were saying but when they stopped speaking, their parents both slumped down on the sofa next to the boys with their face in their hands.

After a few minutes, Daddy Squatpump spoke. His tone was low and solemn,

"Well, if that's the case, we've got to call the RSPCA. Go and get the phone, love." He said to his wife.

23
The Crunch Strikes

Hattie wriggled out of her dog costume. She rolled up the dog head of the costume to make a pillow, and used the body of the costume as a blanket.

The moonlight seeped through the railings of Hattie's kennel as she laid on her back. She could not believe that the twins had ratted out the Galaxiers. Now, she really wouldn't get a chance to speak to Peggy Pigeon. Not only was Gartoid close to finding them, but the Galaxy Garden now had three traitors with Neville and the Squatpump twins! To make matters worse, the RSPCA would soon be on their way too.

It took a long time for Hattie to finally drift off to sleep. Somehow, tomorrow, she had to find a way to speak to Peggy.

"H-E-L-P!"

"Who's there?" Hattie gasped. It was after midnight when she was awoken by a desperate cry.

"H-E-L-P ME." The squeaky voice cried out again. Hattie looked around her kennel anxiously to see where the sound was coming from. She lifted her twin doggy bowl full of biscuits and water - still no clue as to where the voice was coming from. Frustrated, Hattie slammed the bowl on the ground.

"OWWW OWWW," yelled the squeaky voice.

Hattie's eyes widened as she peered into her biscuit bowl. Laid out like a starfish with a bloated tummy the size of the London Wheel, was Missie Mouse.

"Ooooooooowwwwwwwwww," Missie Mouse groaned. She could barely open her eyes. Hattie was confused. Why was Missie Mouse in her kennel? Before Hattie could rush to put on her dog costume, so that Missie Mouse wouldn't recognise her, she heard jangling noises coming from outside. Hurriedly, Hattie pushed open the kennel door. She was right. She did recognise the sound.

Looking up, she saw its rainbow jewels lightly reflecting in the aubergine sky. It soared through the air towards the Galaxy Garden; its ethereal glow, magical and as enchanting as the first time she saw it. *Wait!* Hattie thought, *where was it going?*

BOoOoOoOoOm

The halo crashed through her kennel roof like a lightning strike. It hovered over Hattie's head with its disco lights flashing. Hattie was perplexed.

"Why was the halo here?! The Squatpump twins are the halo bearers. Aren't they?" Hattie said aloud.

"HELP," Missie Mouse continued to cry. Hattie had almost forgotten about Missie. She reached out and gently picked up Missie from the biscuit bowl. The halo continued to hover over Hattie's head, as she nursed Missie in her arms.

Crunch	*Crunch*	*Crunch*
Crunch	*Crunch*	*Crunch*

The early morning sunrise beamed through the damaged kennel roof, forcing Hattie awake. She squinted as she tried to open her eyes. Missie Mouse was sprawled out in the biscuit bowl with her legs apart, and her belly protruding like a pregnant cow. Her cheeks were puffed out like a squirrel storing nuts for hibernation. Hattie eyed Missie, unsure what she was up to.

"**I** [*crunch*] **know** [*crunch*] **it's** [*crunch*] **you** [*crunch*] **Hattie** [*crunch*] [*crunch*] [*crunch*]." Missie boasted.

Hattie's eyes widened in disbelief when she realised that she didn't have her dog costume on! Now Missie Mouse knew that she wasn't Hina the dog. She must have fallen asleep while looking after Missie last night. Missie looked very pleased with herself - like the mouse that got the Camembert. At the top of her voice Missie Mouse announced,

"I know" [*crunch*]

"It's" [*crunch*]

"You Hattie." [*crunch*] [*crunch*] [*crunch*]

"What are you doing?" [*crunch*]

"You're banned honey bun!" [*crunch*] [*crunch*]

"You've got some good biscuits though" [*crunch*]."

"Sssshhhh," Hattie urged.

"Do you have pavement chips?" [*crunch*] [*crunch*]

"Hattie, do **you** have pavement chips?"

Missie Mouse bellowed impatiently.

"Please, Missie Mouse, don't..." Hattie put her index finger to her lips, so Missie Mouse wouldn't shout.

"You're empty-handed, aren't you? Hahahahaha...."

When Missie Mouse was on a food binge, she wouldn't compromise. As Hattie didn't have any food to give to Missie, there was only one thing she could do.

24

Cornrow Bonds

Hattie knelt on the bathroom floor with her head hanging over the side of the bath - such an awkward position! Even though she liked getting her hair styled, washing it was a bit tricky.

Besides, it was her fault, as she was the one who came home with crushed dog biscuits in her hair. She'd told her mum that she'd fallen into Shantis's dog biscuit bowl while they were playing tag in their garden! Given this pathetic excuse, she was lucky that her mum helped her painstakingly remove the biscuit pieces from her hair.

Now the crumbs were gone, Ava turned on the shower head and let the warm water flow onto Hattie's hair. The steam from the shower-head quickly filled the bathroom with the sweet smelling scent of mango and coconut shampoo. Hattie tucked her chin into her chest to stop the suds from running down the side of her face and stinging her eyes. She hated when that happened!

After her mum finished washing her hair, it was time for phase two - hair conditioning! Hattie sat on the closed toilet lid, holding a wet towel around her shoulders, whilst her mum gently towel-dried her now shrunken curls.

Ava lathered conditioner in the palm of her hands and massaged it through Hattie's hair. Then, using a wide-tooth comb, Ava carefully released each knot. Hattie's hair

s-t-r-e-t-c-h-e-d

then instantly

B-o-U-n-C-e-D

back with each stroke.

Ava then ripped open a blue plastic bag and carefully tied it around Hattie's afro, making sure she covered the edges of Hattie's baby hair. The plastic created moisture which helped the conditioner to nourish Hattie's hair. For this to work, however, Hattie had to wait for at least 20 minutes. Usually, she would play with Mia while she waited - yes, with a plastic bag on her head; and yes she always stayed in the house during this process! Well...you can't go out with a bright blue plastic bag on your head, can you?

"I'm just gonna start to fry the fish," Ava said as she headed to the kitchen.

Hattie salivated at the thought of tucking into her mum's fried fish with onions. Especially when it was covered in her mum's special spicy batter. She would eat her fish with a slice of heavenly buttered hard dough bread to soak up all the fish gravy - yum! For now, Hattie had to wait for the conditioner to complete its nourishing magic before tucking into her fish feast. So, she headed to her bedroom, turned on her tv and grabbed her journal.

She started doodling with her scented felt-tips. This was one of her favourite things to do as it helped her think. This time she wrote, 'if only I could get Missie the tastiest pavement chips, in exchange for her setting up a meeting with Peggy Pigeon.' She pondered on it for a moment, then crossed it out. She wrote it again, then crossed it out, thinking it wouldn't work. Instead, she wrote a poem about her beautiful curly hair...

Look at my hair
It's my crown
Each curl twists
With a conditioned kiss

Look at my hair
Its beautiful style
Glistened with oil
and baby hair coils

Look at my hair
Shining like a diamond
It needs special care
So it's strong and vibrant
Look at my hair...

Ava knocked on Hattie's bedroom door. It was time to wash out the conditioner. At last, Hattie thought. She was now closer to getting her hair styled. She put her pen and journal away and headed downstairs.

Hattie sat on a chair in the lounge as Ava squeezed blobs of leave-in conditioner into the palms of her hands and massaged it throughout Hattie's hair. She made sure each hair strand was covered.

Whenever Ava styled Hattie's hair, she liked to tell stories. Today, she told Hattie that afro hair was a way of expressing our culture, creativity and identity. She said, our African ancestors, used it to survive and sometimes they hid rice grains or seeds inside their cornrows. Even though it may have been a small amount, those seeds and grains could feed them if they were captured and forced to move to another slave master's home. And, when they were brave enough, they plaited cornrow patterns in their hair. The plaits were used as maps so they could escape from captivity! Some male African warriors also wore cornrow hair styles which helped to identify which tribe they were from.

Every time Hattie heard these stories, she was amazed. She couldn't believe that she was related to such clever and inspiring African ancestors. Ingenious that our hair was more than just hair! Ava told Hattie, that back in the day, black women moisturised their hair using the oil from fried bacon or butter. This happened, as the texture of our hair, needed moisture to maintain good condition. But nowadays, there were many different hair care brands for our hair type. It wasn't like that in the old days when we had no choice but to use what was available.

As Ava continued with the hair stories, Hattie asked her mum to put her hair up in a bun, with strands falling next to her each ear. Ava finished Hattie's look by tying her yellow and white bandana over the front of her hair; then she slipped Hattie's favourite gold beads on the end of each strand.

As Ava was slipping the gold beads onto Hattie hair, she told Hattie that our ancestors sometimes hid gold in their hair plaits too! Now Hattie felt like royalty. Ava reminded Hattie that afro hair told a story, as did Hattie's hair! From braids to locs, to afro puffs; they were all part of her history and she should be proud of...

every curl!

Ava kissed Hattie on her cheek and gave her a warm long hug after she finished styling her hair. The bond between them in these hair care moments was special. Hattie loved the stories and now felt like a queen with gold in her hair.

"Oh gosh! My fish!" Ava shouted. "My fish is burning!"

As she knew her mum would disappear into a fried fish abyss, Hattie headed to her room to finish her hair style. Facing her mirror, she swiped blobs of gel in circles towards her hair line which made the edges look slick and shiny.

Now Hattie could finish her plan to get back into the Galaxy Garden.

25

Treehouse of Truth

T he morning sun streamed through Hattie's bedroom window reflecting onto her dressing table mirror. Her TV was on a low volume in the background when she heard the McQuibb reporter's name. She stopped and listened.

"It's Carnival weekend here in London, Sunday the 30th of August. The top story this morning; the RSPCA has carried out animal discovery raids across West London. They are acting on intelligence that there are groups of animals being kept in gardens, outhouses, and garages, and the owners are not meeting their needs. Nora-Stink McQuibb reports..."

"Thank you, Jon Did-Fartus. Good morning. I am here at the very place the RSPCA turned up unannounced this morning to rescue groups of animals that have been kept as pets. They've even discovered a woman in her early 30s who kept sheep in her garden

and regularly shaved their wool for her independent business named, 'I've Shaved Wool for These Cardigans' and a man who kept wood pigeons in his coop, which too is strangely named, 'Poop Poop Poop De Coop.'

The RSPCA should be commended for their excellent work here this morning. The animals they have saved will be brought back to the RSPCA base to undergo basic tests and from my understanding, brand new safe and loving homes will be found for all of them. Some will be sent abroad for adoption and others will be sent to children's residential homes to support children in therapeutic settings. Potentially, as it is summer, some animals may be barbec...bar...er, I'm sorry, may have to go to the, the...barbershop and have their furs shaped up and groomed to make them tastier, erm, I mean more... attractive for their new owners.

All hands are on deck for this raid and all animals of course are being handled with care. This is considered a real breakthrough case for the RSPCA!

In due course, there will be a helpline for anyone who has or wants more information about these stray and uncooke...erm, unloved animals. I'm Nora-Stink McQuibb for Channel 300, Stink News, back to you, Jon."

Hattie gasped, threw on her orange duffle coat and snuck out her back door.

Twenty minutes later, she arrived at the Squatpump's house. She was out of breath and sweaty in her thick orange duffle coat. It was August after all, warm enough for just a tee-shirt! She just wasn't thinking!

Hattie stared in horror when she reached the new Galaxy Garden. The furniture was upside down and carelessly strewn around. There was debris everywhere. The dog kennels were smashed into pieces. Hattie's brain whizzed as she turned around quickly, surveying every inch of the Garden. She wished she could see or hear something, but there was nothing and no-one.

She climbed into the Treehouse Office. It was hot and stuffy and smelled of gooey sweat and cat farts.

"It's true," she mumbled to herself as she sat down. "The Galaxy Garden had been raided!"

"Not quite, little girl!" A voice boomed from behind Hattie.

Hattie turned around swiftly.

Standing at the Treehouse entrance with a brown suit jacket and a walking cane, was Neville the Fart-Breath Natter-prat!

"You're a little sneak, aren't you? I knew you were Hina the dog the first time - but this! You've taken it too far, little girly. Dressing up as a dog and eating dog food hahaha, you idiot. I told the Galaxiers Board to keep you in; I needed to see what you were up to but I guess we all know now, don't we?" Neville snarled at Hattie as slimy toad saliva seeped from the corners of his mouth.

Hattie tried to explain it was the Squatpump twins that ratted out the Galaxiers, but Neville sniffed loudly and, in a pompous tone said, "you've probably done me a favour. I'm off to Ireland now; I've come to get my suitcase. My deal with the circus man came through early. He secured my passport and paperwork to travel. I've got a family to go to now Hattie. What have you got?" He asked menacingly.

He hoppity skipped towards the corner of the Office with lashings of Crème Fraiche dripping from every brown self-satisfied pore. He picked up his suitcase and leapt into the next-door neighbour's garden and didn't look back.

Hattie repeated what Natterjack said slowly, "his deal with the circus man?" After pondering what he meant for a few moments, she finally figured it out... Natterjack had planned to turn over the Blue Faced Leicesters to the circus in exchange for a passport to go to Ireland! That's why he was taking photos of them when she first entered into the Galaxy Garden! He needed to prove to the circus man that the Blue Faced Leicesters were alive and well. OMG, Hattie thought. What a double-dealing, crabby face, Creme Fraiche dripping, ugly, warty, pointy teeth, mean, selfish, over tanned traitor! Good job the halo had already matched the Blue Faced Leicester family and they'd left the Galaxy Garden to start their new life. Or, had they? If they hadn't, Hattie thought, why was Natterjack so smug? The thought quickly disappeared from her mind, as out of the corner of her eye, she saw movement. She turned her head slowly. Someone else was there.

She heard what sounded like dirt shuffling on the floor and the desk chair moved slightly, making a dragging noise. Hattie looked over the far corner of the Treehouse Office and saw the back of two heads crawl out from underneath Peggy Pigeon's desk, daring not to look up. When they eventually turned to face her, they spoke quickly in unison, without coming up for air. They blamed their parents for what happened in the Galaxy Garden. They said their parents saw the animals on their garden security camera and alerted the RSPCA. Hattie listened as they continued,

"It's not our fault! They would have been found sooner or later. At least they're safe now and we've secured the pool boy to man our swimming pools. We can't have the pools being dirty, Hattie."

"You little liars!" Hattie said angrily. "I heard you tell them about the Galaxiers. After all the Galaxiers have been through, you didn't keep them safe because you wanted to keep your pool boys?! WOW!"

"Well, Hattie, you shoved them to the side because you wanted to sit at your friend's house and drink fruit juice. The Galaxiers will be fine; they always are." They rolled their eyes again in unison.

"Now I know, that's why the halo came to me last night! You Pump Squat idiots! Even the halo knows that you're both traitors."

"It's Squatpump actually, Hattie."

26

Chips and Cheese Pave the Way

Hattie dressed up as a mouse so she could get into
Vinnie's Cheese Bites, the swanky underground mice
jazz club with the best cheese in town. She wore an Alice
band with mice ears and a long silver dress with a glitter
tail that trailed behind her. Black pencil whiskers were
drawn on her cheeks and costumed mouse hands covered
her fingers. She had been to Vinnie's Cheese Bites with
Howard Horse before when he secured business for the
Mice Boys.

She stepped onto glossy white marble floor as
she entered the club. The smell of cheese-filled culinary
delights, perfumed the air. The club exuded an age old
café ambiance. White vintage chairs, stencilled around
the frames in gold, were neatly tucked under tables with
reverse scroll-legs. Crisp white tablecloths were expertly
folded at the corners and spread over each table. Each
table had a candle lantern placed in their centre which
provided a warm glow of light throughout the club.

The audience was packed with finely attired rodents. The men wore three-piece suits with colourful cravats, while the ladies glittered in shimmering ball gowns and the highest crystal glass stilettos Hattie had ever seen.

The singers belted out their improvised scat to the accompanying music of the 3-piece jazz band. Everyone cheered after each band member completed their solo performances.

Hattie was so far back that she couldn't see the stage clearly; but she heard the music stop suddenly. A squeaky voice magnified on the mic. It looked like someone was proposing, as they were down on one knee. The lady must have said yes, because within seconds, glasses clinked, and celebratory cheers resounded. Everyone started canoodling to a slow romantic song which was being sung by the person who'd proposed...

Four-teen days from now
I'll walk you down the aisle We'll waltz the same song in
style Hold-ing hands
Making swee-eet memo-ries
In four-teen days from now...

The man kissed his future bride. They hugged and walked off the stage, hand in hand to shouts of 'congratulations' and 'good luck' from the audience.

Meanwhile, security guards dressed in black suits busied themselves trying to keep order. The butlers wore gold gloves with pristine tuxedos and served uncorked wine and hot plates of food. They were assisted by smiling waitresses, who wore black tuxedo dresses. They made sure everyone was being served. Hattie was distracted by the mounds of food cooking on an open fire. She heard it sizzle and pop. A waiter walked elegantly in a straight line, balancing a food platter precariously in one hand, with the other hand behind his back.

There was so much going on that it was difficult for Hattie to see. She had to find Vincent to ask for Howard Horse's phone number, as she'd lost it. Although Hattie didn't know whether Howard had been taken in the raid, she wanted to try and get help. Vincent was her only chance of starting a rescue mission, as she didn't know anyone else who knew about the Galaxy Garden. She was hoping that Vincent could contact Howard to help her to rescue the Galaxiers.

When Hattie got closer to the main stage, she saw several mice entering the stage. There was a throng of applause as they walked on. Hattie could see that they had already charmed the audience before they had even squeaked a note. They were wearing blue velvet double-breasted suits, purple bow ties and black patent shoes.

Before the mice began to sing, two of them disappeared backstage and returned with the newly engaged couple. The audience clapped and cheered. All Hattie could see were their silhouettes. One looked very small and the other, was tall with curious feet. Frills fluttered from the hips of the taller silhouette who also appeared to have a gigantic snout. The smaller one had to hold their hand in the air to reach the taller silhouette. They were oddly mismatched! The lights dimmed as the taller silhouette took the mic and began to speak,

"Thank you sooooo much for your love and kisses. I haf vaited a berry long time for this moment in my life. I am soooo happy. I can't vait to be Mrs Vynegarr, The Goose Mice Boy."

"Mrs Vynegarr The Goose Mice Boy!" Hattie mouthed the name slowly. Why did it sound familiar? But... wait. Hattie's eyes widened! Vynegarr and a Mice Boy - getting married? But how? Why? It couldn't be...

What would their babies look like? Hattie shook the vision from her mind. She would have to think about that later. Maybe, just maybe, the animals on stage were the Galaxiers. Hattie wasn't fully convinced but she didn't think twice and barged her way towards the stage.

"Excuse me, excuse me," Hattie screeched, desperate to be heard. "Is that VYNEGARR?" If it was her, she had to let her know the Galaxy Garden had been raided. She stood in front of the stage and looked up. OMG! It was! It really was. It was the Galaxiers!

"Hello, HELLO!" She bawled. They ignored her and continued speaking to the audience. Hattie clambered onto the stage. No sooner had her right foot met her left on the raised platform, than the Galaxy Garden Brummie Chicken Security Guards blocked her path.

"Not you!" They said together. "Why do you keep going round the Wrekin, bab? You're like the number 8 buzz on the inner circle, going round and round the island."

"I've got something importan—"

"You keep popping back to have a mooch when you deffed us off. Ta-ra ra abit. TA-RA!" They said indignantly. The conjoined chickens opened their three legs and wings at the same time, trying to block Hattie from going any further. She folded her arms in protest trying to figure out how to 'outfox' (hehehe) their dumbo chicken wings. She took two steps back, bent down and darted through their legs. They struggled to keep their balance as they tried to close both legs to stop her, but Hattie was through. She crashed into the huddle of mice on the stage. The audience gasped as she tried to dodge the Brummie chickens, who chased after her.

"Are you kidding me?" squeaked a voice.

"YOU! You left us," heckled another. Vynegarr, the Goose looked behind to see what was causing the commotion. After all, this was her engagement celebration. She dropped her mic and walked towards Hattie.

"Get up!" she shouted. Hattie did as she was told. The Brummie Chickens watched.

"Ze Mice Boys are working here. We're earning cheese to-a go-a back-a to ze Galaxy Garden tonighta. We do not have time for zis!"

"I know. I know, but the Galaxy Garden, well...it's gone!" Hattie said sheepishly.

"Get off the stage," an audience member shouted.

"No, I can't!" Hattie shouted back. She turned to The Mice Boys and whispered, "the Galaxy Garden is gone. The RSPCA raided it and took everyone!"

The Mice Boys rolled their eyes, convinced that Hattie was trying to get into their good books again.

"Missie Mouse told us, you were Hina the Dog all along Hattie! You lied, as well as abandoned us. We've told you, we're with the Squatpump twins now."

The Mice Boys started to usher Hattie off the stage.

"No! I promise I'm not lying...wait, guys, listen..." Hattie pleaded.

"WAIT! WAIT! WAIT! WAIT! WAIT!" A high-pitched shrill resounded through the crowd of mice.

"WAIT! What if she's got pavement chips?" Everyone stopped. Then, after a short bout of silence,

"For goodness sake, what a farce!" Vynegarr the Goose said.

"Listen, if *she's* got pavement chips, she won't be lying. Trrrrrust me, I'll know."

A little mouse with pink shoes wearing a candy print dress stepped forward holding onto a half-eaten chicken wing in one hand. Her mouth was covered in barbecue sauce. She waved the chicken wing about as she spoke.

"Go on, Hattie. Do you have pavement chips?"

Hattie reached under her long silver dress and pulled out a handful of pavement chips from her dungaree pocket. She held them mid-air, like Simba being introduced to the pride.

"Oh my God, Oh my God! OOOOOHHHH my God! OMG! She's not lying! She's not lying, guys. She da truth sister!" Missie Mouse shrieked hopping about like she was on hot coals.

"I'm telling you the truth, Missie! While you guys were working, the Galaxy Garden got raided. The Galaxiers are gone!" Missie Mouse paced back and forth taking a chip from Hattie's hand with each turn, chewing ferociously with every bite.

"Waiter," Missie hollered. "Give me the most the scrumlicious piece of blue stanky cheese you can find."

A waiter stepped forward and handed Missie a neatly wrapped cheese parcel from his serving tray. Missie grabbed it, stuffed it in her shoe and bellowed, "this way, Hattie, C'MON everyone!"

27
Aviator Chickenese

"What you saying? I thought you said she was HERE Booker!" Man Like Dlux asked in a raised voice.

"Don't you think I got advice fam? Hear me out. Remember we came here for the Smart Pigeon Contest with quiz master Hattie, and we won the Golden Love Bread for our prize? Hattie told me she got the bread from here in her garden fam."

"So what, blood?" Man Like Dlux questioned.

"You know bruv, you only get *that* bread with Pigeon Paper! Meaning, she might know something about the destruction of Pigeon Palace my guy."

"Are you fo real?! Are you saying what I think you're saying blood? Cuz my wife and I bought the last gluten free Golden Love Bread. I didn't even think of that you know."

"I know man. I remember seeing it in your coop man. Your wife always talked about it being an investment for your future children but yo, tell me the truth bruv; how long you been separated man? I ain't seen her in a minute."

Man Like Dlux sat on the floor and put his head in hands. "I didn't want to tell you... but—"

"Well, where is she bro? Is everything ok?" Booker asked.

Dlux hesitated, then confessed, "bro, she's been missing for 9 months man. 9 months you know Booker. I want my wife back man."

"Missing? But I thought you said?...Why didn't you tell me man?" Booker said.

"I thought I'd be able to find her bruv but I can't, I *just* can't find her man."

"Who's got her bruv? I've got a man dat can deal with this right now, let me help you, yeah?"

"It's not that simple bruv. I don't even want to get into it." Man Like Dlux replied.

"Cool, cool, cool, cool...well, I'm here for you man and it's a good job I brought you here ennit? Think about dis, yeah? If your wife bought the last Golden Love Bread...that means, she was *definitely* here man! No-one has kept their bread as long your wife man, trust me. There's got to be a clue somewhere, you get me?"

"True, true, true..." Man Like Dlux agreed.

"C'mon bruv, let's go get your wife and give her back her piece of *gluten free* Golden Love Bread, yeah?"

"At a time like this, you got jokes Booker?" Dlux shook his head in disbelief.

Booker laughed, "what bruv? You keep saying you eat gluten free but your belly looks like a gluten belly to me."

"What?! Are you mad bruv? You see this here? This is a washboard bruv with packs on packs, yeah?" Dlux sucked his teeth. They both laughed and began to search the ruins of Galaxy Garden Rosebush HQ at Hattie's house.

They flew into the kitchen and landed on the central island. On the kitchen counter, were pictures of multi-coloured circles, photos of the Queen, mathematical equations and sketches. Booker and Man Like Dlux inspected the paperwork closely. An invitation read,

Dear Professor Manderblythen,

The Queen wishes to extend her gratitude to you for your magnificent Sinkatraon Halo Crown I. The Queen was most elated to wear your handmade Halo. Her Majesty's special day is soon approaching, and she would be honoured to wear it again.

In light of the circumstances, I am to send Her Majesty's best wishes to you and your highly skilled team in anticipation of the development of yet another outstanding and innovative Sinkatron Halo II.

May I take this opportunity to cordially invite you to Her Majesty's Ninety Fifth Birthday Celebration on 15th October at Balmoral Castle, Aberdeenshire. Please refer to the enclosed invitation for further details.

The Queen very much looks forward to seeing you again.

RSVP

Miss Felicity Hornbeam-Richards, MVO
Deputy Correspondence Coordinator

Who on earth was Professor Manderblythen and why would an invitation from the Queen be in the Galaxy Garden kitchen?

Booker surveyed the kitchen. It looked like a mighty explosion had been detonated in there. Cupboards hung loosely off their hinges, kitchen draws were left open - most were broken and utensils strewn on the floor covered with rubble.

Booker and Man Like Dlux kicked the rubble aside in order to continue the search. They looked everywhere but found nothing significant until—

"Hear wah me a sey, right? Time is against mi yuh know. Mi a stay here in a this Galaxy place fi wait fi dem stupid likkle thieving animals to come back. Two weeks past and not one! Not even a likkle ant come in here."

Booker and Man Like Dlux watched as a short stout caucasian looking man strolled into the kitchen. He had on a white lab coat. His large shiny forehead reflected under the kitchen lights. He stood next to the island surrounded by six seagulls.

"Yuh see dis design here?' He picked up some papers and waved it around aggressively in the seagulls' faces, flicking the edge of the papers with the back of his hand.

"This is a BRAND NEW design. If I don't get back my halo, unu, unu, unu, unu, unu AND UNU, will have to sacrifice yuh holiday pay and help me put this together. Do you hear me? Now, gwan an guh look fi de cheeky crooked thieving fools and don't bother coming back without me tings! Me se GWAN WEH!" Gartoid shooed the seagulls out of the kitchen.

Booker and Man Like Dlux watched as Gartoid walked over to the fridge, opened it and took out a lemon and a bowl containing a plump raw chicken. He walked to the sink area and turned on the tap. He rummaged around in several cupboards before he pulled out a knife. He then found some foil and a baking tray laying them aside. From a great height, he raised the knife and karate chopped the lemon in half. He took one half of the lemon in each hand and carefully squeezed the juice all over the raw chicken. He then rinsed the chicken under running water, humming Bob Marley's Three Little Birds in the process. Drying his hands on a nearby towel, he patted the pockets of his white coat and pulled out what looked like a cluster of sparkling gems. He placed the gems into the piece of foil, wrapped them tightly and stuffed the foil inside the chicken.

He walked to the Galaxy Garden oven and fiddled with the knobs until the flames ignited. He placed the chicken on the tray and popped it onto the top shelf of the oven and closed the glass oven door. He then washed his hands and went back to the kitchen island to set an egg timer. He clasped his hands with glee, and sauntered out of the kitchen.

Man Like Dlux noticed Booker salivating as he watched the chicken glow through the oven door.

He whispered to Booker, "yo, stay focused blood. We're here to try and find my wife, yeah?"

Booker raised his wings, not even looking at Dlux and said, "yeah, cool, cool, cool cool..." Booker then flew down from their hiding spot, to face the oven.

"Gosh man!" Man Like Dlux huffed as he followed Booker. "We need to stay out of sight." His words fell on deaf ears. He eyed Booker closely and knew that he would now have to nurse Booker's Aviator Chickenese affliction.

He'd seen Booker's condition manifest itself before. It happened whenever Booker saw a chicken and was so at ease that he couldn't stop staring at the chicken. That's why Booker couldn't watch Man Like Dlux perform at any establishment that had chicken on their menu, because he would become so transfixed by the chicken, he would have a bout of paralysis for hours.

Dlux watched as Booker pitifully dribbled all over his clothes, transfixed by the glow from the oven. Man Like Dlux grabbed a piece of kitchen towel from nearby and placed it under Booker's chin to catch the first of a pool of his dribble. He then lifted Booker, placing him into an open cupboard in full view of the oven to keep him out of Gartoid's sight while he continued looking for his wife.

28

Blue Cheese Wonder

Hattie, Dr Gertrude Vynegarr, the Brummie Chickens and The Mice Boys hid at the back entrance of what used to be the Rosebush HQ in Hattie's garden. To keep them out of sight, Missie Mouse led the group via secret routes that only she knew about.

They needed the help of the Wonder Warren Cooperative Society who lived underneath the Galaxy Garden to help them rescue the captured Galaxiers.

They arrived at the Galaxy Garden apple tree behind the HQ and stopped. Missie Mouse fiddled inside her shoe and pulled out a squashed piece of garlic blue cheese. YUK!! It stunk! She laid it on the ground close to the tree, and stood back, signalling the group to hush. They waited in silence for a full two minutes before...

bOoM bOoM BoOm De De BoOm

A hole suddenly appeared in the ground and a giant blue-haired rabbit with long blonde hair, erupted from the hole causing a meteoric crater in the ground. It wore a red jacket and a neck tie labelled, Wonder Warren Garden Porter.

"Ooooooh weeeee! Who left that stanky cheese up here?! You know I can't stand that smell - go on, get it outta here and tell me where you're going!" the rabbit demanded, holding its nose in the air.

Missie Mouse quickly picked up the stanky piece of cheese and shoved it back in her shoe.

"Rabbit Hole, ONE ONE ONE please," Missie requested. The rabbit nodded and beckoned the group to follow him.

One by one, they stepped into the rabbit hole elevator. The porter rotated his ears 270 degrees and the elevator doors closed.

"My name is Caramel Buck." The rabbit said. "I'm new here." He sniffed at the group twitching his nose. "They still ain't sorted out my new uniform, you know. This one is borrowed. It really gets on my fur." He sniffed again, smiling to himself.

"It's like buying a ring doughnut. I mean, why the carrot sticks does it have a hole in it?! JESUS! *I think I was robbed you know. I didn't get the full doughnut!"*

Caramel Buck was from South Carolina. He spoke very quickly and made little sense.

"It's like the other day, I was minding my own business walking down the Warren here and an ant came up to me and asked where the eye doctor was, because he tried to roll a rock but it clipped his left eye and now he's gotta lot a floaters. Poor thang! Thinks we have a fly infestation in the Warren office. Hasn't been the same since; so I asked him, why do you think I would know where the eye doctor is located? You know what he told me? He said, carrots can make you see better, right? I said, yes they can make *humans* see better and they are what *I* like to eat. So, he says, well, show me the way to go, to get my eye checked out. I was so mad! I mean, I was sooooooo, I mean, *really* mad. I don't know why people get mistaken about this; I ain't got a human body,

I'm a rabbit. Yes, there's scientific evidence for humans, that carrots make 'em see better but please be quiet, there's no real evidence of that for us. So I politely said, listen here...God put the first ant on earth right, he was adamANT! *Ha he Ha he...*Go be adamANT some where else, and pray your wife isn't getting too close to the ten-ANTS in that tree you live in. We wouldn't want her to accidentally on purpose but accidentally on purpose cause the whole world to get *ANT-sy! Ha he Ha he Ha.* He was *so* rude!

Then he shouted at me, 'thanks for nothing! Keep calm and car-rot on!' Do you know how offensive that is? It's like saying to me I'm a hot cross bunny when I ask for the right carrot delivery. Honestly, I get grey hares thinking about this stuff. Ya know what a mean...?"

Missie Mouse replied eagerly, "yeah, I do actually; someone at Vinne's Cheese Bites told me to rename the Mice banquets, *Hamster-dam* Parties."

"Exactly!" Caramel Buck replied. They both looked at each other and chuckled.

"You don't happen to have any of those doughnuts with you, do you?" Missie ventured. Never missing an opportunity for free food - even in a crisis.

"STOP TALKING MISSIE MOUSE," the group hollered. Missie ignored them.

"Cuz if you do have any difficulty, you know, eating them, *I'm your girl!* The ring doesn't bother me, to be honest. I love strawberry icing covered ring doughnuts and hundreds and thousands covered ring doughnuts. The humans are really creative these days. They have all sorts of tasty toppi..." Missie spouted.

Caramel Buck laughed as he twisted his ears again to open the elevator doors. He stepped aside to let the group out,

"I'll *hare* that in mind," Caramel Buck winked.

Caramel Buck didn't have much company being the elevator porter for the Wonder Warren Cooperative Society because he lived underground, separate from the Galaxiers. They didn't get much sun for most of the year and were thinner and pastier than the skinniest Galaxier. To top it off, they were all vegans and did not mix with carnivores, as they wanted to sustain their way of life.

Their flagship online company, So Very Very Vegan, sustained their existence. They shared tips and information on their website about living a healthy plant-based life. They had lived side by side with the Galaxiers in relative peace. This was the first time they'd been called upon to help the Galaxiers. They believed some of the Galaxiers' ethos matched their own - apart from the rabbit porters who inducted baby rabbits to help grow their hundreds of fruits and vegetables. In return for their time, they were able to take back one overgrown knobbly carrot to their Warren.

They were only helping the Galaxiers because they saw the Galaxy Garden being attacked on their cameras. They wouldn't ordinarily intervene as the Galaxiers had the powerful halo which they had watched with great intrigue and interest. Caramel Buck was the American contingent sent to learn the Wonder Warren's extraordinary way of life, so he could transport it back to America to help save their planet. That was the reason he was so chatty - far from home, with no sun!

Before Gertrude left the elevator, she gave Caramel Buck a celebratory meal box from the party bag she had been given at Vinnie's when she got engaged.

"There dear," she said, "enjoy your dinner tonight with zis."

Caramel Buck inspected the label on the celebratory box, which read: Carmagnola Carbonara. The elevator doors began to close as Caramel banged and shouted from the inside.

"JESUS!! What have you given me

this for, lady? Carmagnola ARE MY COUSINS, I can't eat cooked rabbit, lady... LADY?!" His voice trailed off into a muted scream as the elevator descended.

The group sauntered past the Wonder Warren reception. Hattie noticed a sign which read,

'WONDER WARREN PRIVATE RESIDENCE.'

As they walked through the tunnels burrowed out of soil, they noticed several chamber rooms with numerous rabbits busying themselves, carrying food, pushing trolleys and managing post. It looked like a full business operation was in motion.

They approached a door labelled, 'Gaffer's Wonder Office.' Missie Mouse, far too impatient, repeatedly knocked on the door. A few moments later, a rabbit porter let them in.

A round wooden table was positioned in the middle of the room. Rabbits in blue suits were seated on wooden chairs. On the table was an assortment of vegetables; beetroot leaves, carrot tops, celery and large jugs of water.

Missie Mouse broke away from the group and, forgetting her manners, leapt onto the table. She began rummaging through the vegetables hurriedly. After finding what she wanted, she popped her head above the rim of the plate, holding a piece of celery in one hand. With the other hand, she carefully, reached inside her pink shoes and pulled out the piece of stinky garlic blue cheese. Sticking out her tongue, she wetted the blue cheese with some spit before sticking it onto the celery. She tried to take a bite but winced as the celery was too hard to chew with her baby teeth.

She wanted desperately to swallow the cheese so the rabbit porters wouldn't throw her out for stinking out the room and bringing non-vegan friendly food into their Warren. But, she began to tremble as a dark shadow towered over her. Her eyes widened in terror and disappeared into the back of her head as she began to rise from the vegetable bowl by her feet! Oh No! Someone was lifting her but she couldn't see who. For a change, Missie couldn't speak as she was balancing the blue cheese and the celery stick between her teeth -

upside down! Whoever it was, airlifted her to the manager's chair and gently placed her down.

"Come, come" the voice boomed, "I saw you on the cameras."

29

Pigeon Planet

"What a relief to have our matriarch safe and well." Dr. Vynegarr announced.

Everyone cheered and clapped with excitement. Hattie was so happy to see Peggy again, and Missie... well let's just say, the blood is still rushing to her head from being held upside down facing a plate of veggies.

"Alright, alright, my fellow Galaxiers. You can climb off me now and watch my nail polish. Girl, you know I don't get my nails chipped! Hahaha, yes, it's wonderful to see you too....and you. It's so good to have neighbours you can count on isn't it? The Wonder Warren and the Galaxiers don't really share that much in common but are here when we need them. It was the only place I could come to when I found out the New Galaxy Garden had been raided." Peggy stopped and eyed Hattie.

"And you Hattie," Peggy stopped smiling, "we need to have a talk, don't we?"

Peggy stepped away from the excitement and beckoned Hattie to follow her. They left the office and walked along the Warren towards the elevator.

"I knew dear, I knew you were Hina the dog and I also knew dear, all about Neville Natterjack. He's always been selfish! He'll be back anyway. What I didn't know is that you were going to turn your back on us Galaxiers. Friendship is something very dear to my heart love, and I know being the halo bearer has its responsibilities, but anything that gives you any sort of power comes with that dear.

I know Hattie, that the halo is a new concept and your first duty came in the midst of a crisis. Remember, I came to Mia's house and asked you to come back to the Galaxy Garden? I know the timing was all wrong for you dear, as you were desperately missing Mia. But Hattie, there is something you must understand. We can all feel lost or out of place sometimes but I believe if we just continue to help each other, and stay open to new possibilities, even when we feel unsure dear, we can always find a place to belong. That's why we had to move to the Squatpump twins. You gave us little choice. When they lived at your house and were the halo bearers, they never left us stranded. They always came to our aid. Hattie, I can see this is something you may struggle with, so my question to you is, what are you doing here?"

"Well, I pretended to be Hina the Dog, so I could explain everything to you. Neville Natterjack has always been mean to me, and I was trying to be a good friend by letting the Galaxiers know that he was being mean to them too. I promise I have not said anything to anyone about the Galaxy Garden. I never broke that promise."

They reached the elevator and stepped in.

"Caramel Buck, take us up to the Chamber Lounge, please." Peggy commanded.

"Sure thing Ma'am," he replied with his dazzling smile.

"Well, Hattie dear, you need to know that I too have responsibilities. It's a lot to manage these Galaxiers, my lovely. It's tiring and I barely get a moment to myself but I keep going, so I can help those I now call my family, because, that is what they are now Hattie. The Galaxiers are my family dear—"

"Miss...Ma'am. Excuse me. Miss Peggy, you've got some a-coo-stics haven't you?" Caramel chortled. Peggy didn't reply. Hattie was slightly bewildered and unsure about Caramel's sense of humour. The elevator stopped and the doors opened. Hattie and Peggy stepped out into the chamber lounge.

"Stay safe now, *Merci boo coo, coo coo!* Get it? *Coo coo.* That's the sound pigeons make, right?"

"Caramel Buck," Peggy Pigeon said indignantly but with a wry smile. "Haven't you got to hip-hop somewhere else?"

"Peggy my dear, you look im-pegg-able today, ha he ha he."

His shoulders jiggled and he breathed in after every 'ha he ha he' which made him sound like an asthmatic donkey.

"Oh, I don't *car-rot* what you say Caramel. I'm always *im-pegg-able!* Hattie? *Let-tuce* pray, for his hare line. Mr thinks he's so *hop* stuff. I'll have a word with Rabbit Resources Department to get him reappointed to the *hare* force. Hahahaha."

"Listen! Listen here, I don't wanna ruffle no feathers, but I can see the *feather* forecast is, pretty *fowl*," Caramel Buck chuckled his asthmatic donkey laugh again which made Hattie smirk. She just noticed that he had a single buck tooth which gathered spit with each asthmatic laugh.

"Oh no, of course not. You're the fast and *furriest iv* aren't you? No bunny compares to you!"

Peggy rolled her eyes and tittered. Hattie never knew Peggy had a sense of humour, never mind ribbing a fast talking rabbit from America.

"Come on, join in. Tell him Hattie." Peggy urged.

"No speaka de English." Hattie said trying to be funny.

"No, no, Hattie. Say something bad *and* funny. Join in dear."

"Wow! Erm.... Me sey gwan!"

"That's it dear! Tell him to go away," Peggy laughed.

"Nice *haring* around with you both." Caramel said. They all laughed and made funny faces at each other, until the elevator door closed.

Peggy and Hattie walked through the Chamber Lounge and continued their talk.

"I love, love, love Caramel Buck; such a warm spirit, isn't he Hattie? Haha ok, as I was saying; I try my best, but truth is Hattie, I want to be reunited with my husband. I feel lost sometimes too, you know. My husband and I became separated in the Pigeon Palace robbing months ago. We were the King and Queen of

Pigeon Planet, a small pigeon community in central London. We had our own currency, shops and everything. When we lived in Pigeon Palace, we had butlers, cleaners, you name it dear, but it was destroyed. My dear husband went out for a Royal engagement one evening, and whilst he was gone, someone broke into our palace and kidnapped me.

They held me for ransom in the London caves for 1 million Pigeon Papers. That was the entire cost of our palace Hattie! My husband couldn't get the money together because they destroyed our beautiful palace. There was nothing left! I was caged for weeks dear, eating hideous wheat flour bread pieces; it didn't agree with me dear. Gluten-free suits me best," Peggy smiled.

"Hattie, I pooped so much in the cage, it began to overflow. They didn't like it, and winced every time they looked at me. After all dear, the Queen doesn't poop! I was so embarrassed; but one day, they decided to open the cage to clean it out. I flew for my life, dear. My wings flapped so hard I almost collapsed, hahaha.

The Galaxy Gardeners Rescue Association was a charity I supported for years in Pigeon City. So, when I too became estranged, I decided to set up a branch of my own and called it, 'The Galaxy Garden.' On my travels, I met so many estranged animals who have now joined. It's grown significantly in just over six months dear. The halo was an added bonus, to be honest.

The halo came about because Missie Mouse's family stole it from Buckingham Palace and brought it back here. While we all admired it, we kept it in the Galaxy Garden safe, ready to return it the next day. When Neville Natterjack went to retrieve it the following morning from our safe...poof! It had disappeared. A week later, the halo fell from the sky when the Squatpump twins were playing in the garden. What we witnessed after that was pure magic, dear. One of the goats was reunited with their long-lost uncle, just like that! That's when we realised the Galaxy Garden was somewhere special and we needed special children like you to help us. Those Squatpump twins helped us reunite over 50 animal families Hattie. I love those boys. They're truly wonderful."

Peggy clasped her hands together in pure delight as she talked about the Squatpump twins.

"Wow!" Hattie said, amazed.

"You see Hattie, the Galaxy Garden has been destroyed because of Gartoid. He wants his halo back. But we don't know how to give it back to him. It's got a mind of its own. Now, we have the added problem that the halo is very useful to us. It's helping to unite so many animals who've been separated.

Anyway, I know who's caused the Galaxy Garden to be destroyed, dear. It's all Gartoid! He's done this to us, and we're going to have to work triple hard to rebuild it."

"It wasn't Gartoid," Hattie blurted out. "It was —"

She quickly covered her mouth with her hands. She couldn't believe that all this time she was trying to speak to Peggy Pigeon and now, here she was standing in front of her and she couldn't actually say who destroyed the Galaxy Garden.

She wanted to tell Peggy that the Squatpump twins were responsible for the RSPCA raids, but Peggy thought so highly of them, she probably wouldn't believe her.

30
Chamber Lounge SPECTACLE

Hattie and Peggy suddenly fell silent. They leaned their heads to one side and listened. They could hear screams and yelps coming from above. It sounded like something was rolling around on the roof. They glanced up. Suddenly, a small crack started to appear from the centre of the ceiling, quickly spanning outwards. Another crack then followed, this time from the left corner snaking across the entire ceiling. Specs of dust began to float downwards lingering in the air. The noise grew louder and now resounded into the chamber lounge. Hattie and Peggy quickly stepped back, then darted for cover as the ceiling sunk inwards and came tumbling down.

CRRRAAAASSSSHHHH!!!!

Gartoid and Booker suddenly fell into the chamber lounge from a giant hole in the ceiling. They tussled and wrestled each other on the floor, overturning and breaking furniture. Booker, briefly got the better of Gartoid and shoved him. Gartoid fell backwards, bashing the back of his head on the arm of a sofa. Booker flew onto Gartoid's stomach and repeatedly pecked at him with his vicious beak.

"Give it to me!" Booker shouted.

"Gwan. Come out a mi face!" Gartoid yelled, grabbing Booker's beak.

"It's mine blood!" Booker yelled back.

"No, man! Yuh likkle thieving bwoy. This is mine, I did mek it!" Gartoid clapped back.

Hurriedly, Hattie and Peggy Pigeon slipped out of the lounge as the fight got rowdier. They practically sprinted to the gaffer's office to alert the rabbit porters and remaining Galaxiers about the fight. Hattie explained that Gartoid Manderblythen and Booker were scuffling in the chamber lounge. Peggy spoke quickly as she was panicking. She had never seen Gartoid before. She felt confused, "well, how did he...how did he know about the Wonder Warren? And, Booker? Booker the pigeon lawyer? No way! He's with Gartoid, our enemy?

That's...? But how do you know Booker, Hattie? You must be mistaken dear! It just can't be."

Peggy paused. She had to think quickly.

"Right, Missie Mouse, take The Mice Boys and go and keep an eye on them. Quickly! GO!"

Missie Mouse and The Mice Boys hurried through the tunnels, as the sound of the fight resounded through the walls crafted out of soil. When they arrived, they could hardly catch their breath. Missie looked as if she was about to keel over with exhaustion. The rest of The Mice Boys were bent over with their tongues hanging out, panting like dehydrated tigers. Eventually, they laid on their bellies and peeked under the door.

There was a unified sharp intake of breath as they saw Gartoid and Booker playing tug and war with a golden roasted chicken. They tugged and pulled the chicken back and forth, up and down, around and across.

"Me sey let go, you pigeon fool!" Gartoid cried out.

"Nah, man!" Booker shouted back.

The tussling became more intense as they wrestled the chicken in so many directions that it began to shred and flake all over the floor until it split.

"AAAAAAHHHHHHHH!"

They both screamed as they fell onto the floor. One held a quarter of the chicken breast and the other held the remains of a thigh bone.

Giblets flew through the air, a wing there, a leg here, splattered liver everywhere. Pieces of foil littered every corner of the lounge and multi-coloured gems sprayed from the chicken, pinging like hail stones as they hit the floor. Frantically, Gartoid scampered around the room, gathering the scattered gems and stuffing them into his lab coat pocket.

"Me can't believe this. These are my gems! What did I do to deserve this? I was just trying to get what's rightfully mine."

During Gartoid's gem fest frenzy, Booker leant against the sofa, calm as a millpond, tearing open a piece of French bread he'd pulled from his trouser leg. He filled it with pieces of shredded chicken he'd rescued with his beak.

He pulled a napkin from his pocket and tucked it into his shirt collar under his chin. Stretching out his wing, he lifted his tie and threaded it through the button holes on his shirt. He surveyed the room for a brief moment, before licking his lips and biting into his chicken baguette. He watched as panic stricken Gartoid continued the hunt for his gems stones.

31
Wobbles, Squabbles and Cobbled Rabble

"THERE YOU ARE, blood!" Man Like Dlux said as he flew through the hole caused by Gartoid and Booker's fight. His sliders fell, as usual, from each claw, one after the other, before he landed in the Chamber.

"What you doing in here Booker? Where you get that French bread from?" He asked, as he retrieved and slipped his sliders back on.

Booker, preoccupied with enjoying his food, took a minute to reply. Man Like Dlux hesitated for a fleeting second, surveying the room before the penny finally dropped! To hide his shame, Booker quickly retorted,

"Come man, let me give you some. You ain't eaten lunch anyway, bruv. Come, man," he chided.

Dlux asked, "aren't you over this Aviator Chickenese thing yet man?" As he spoke, a juicy piece of mangled chicken leg caught his eye.

He licked his lips and said, "you should be, but not just yet though – nothing like a free lunch with my brethren."

When Gartoid managed to gather all of his gems, he stopped for a moment and eyed the room suspiciously. As he secreted the last gem in his pocket, he looked up again. This time, in disbelief, as he observed the two pigeons eating while he was afflicted with the near death hysteria of rummaging for his gems. He gritted his teeth and marched over to Dlux.

"Who is you?" He demanded.

Dlux immediately dashed his chicken baguette to the side which rolled on the floor. Due to Dlux's eyes being at the front now, instead of at the sides, he faced Gartoid, head on and yelled back,

"Nah. Who are you bruv? Matter of fact, where's my wife, G? WHERE'S MY WIFE?"

"I don't know what you're talking about brudda. I don't know nuttin about your wife. You have my halo? You tek it?" Gartoid towered over Dlux, who stood on the tip of his claws in an attempt to measure up.

"Nah, bruv. I don't know anything about that. Step back, yeah? Anyways, what halo?"

"Your pigeon friend," Gartoid said pointing at Booker, whose only interest was chomping on his baguette, "is fighting me brudda. I'm just heating up my gems to change their pigment, you get me? You can bring out a new colour when you apply high heat to them. I need to try and do this to mek another halo, fe de Queen - yuh see me? I would usually blast them with me own fire at my Fortuna Sinkatron Lab but I had to make a likkle adjustment today and me end up in some fight with dis pigeon here." He pointed menacingly at Booker.

Dlux gave Gartoid a wry smile before retrieving his baguette. He bit into it furiously, realising that Gartoid knew nothing about the whereabouts of his wife.

He observed Gartoid closely and said, "Gems? Is dat you blood?"

"Well, me nuh have no choice. Some likkle hanimal thief me 'alo and I can't find where dem put it. Yuh see me?"

Small clumps of soil hung from the edges of the crater in the ceiling from where Gartoid and Booker fell in. Gartoid walked back and forth scrutinising the hole. He was contemplating how he could get back to his make-shift lab that he'd set up in the Galaxy Garden kitchen. But the hole was probably too high for him to reach. He flapped his hands in annoyance and retorted,

"How mi fe get out now?"

When looking out into the garden, he noticed the sky was beginning to change from light blue to midnight purple, then it slowly became an aubergine colour.

32
The Trumpets of Light

T he Mice boys who had remained silent during the entire chicken spat, and who continued to peek from under the door, without warning, were blown off balance as a gust of wind descended into the chamber. The sound of jangling bells grew louder and the wind picked up speed. The shadow of flashing lights started to get brighter and bolder.

Booker and Man Like Dlux stopped chomping on their baguette and peered into the sky. Their eyes widened and their mouths fell open revealing chewed up chicken and French bread, which slipped out of their beaks and onto their chests. Gartoid yanked off his glasses and gawped into the sky. An evil grin slowly began to form on his face. It got wider until he burst into giddy hysterical laughter. He hopped around the Chamber Lounge, yelping and screaming with joy.

"YES! A me dat! Yuh see me! Hahahahaha. That's MY halo!" Gartoid said. The halo soared towards the Chamber Lounge. Its bright coloured gems glistened against the aubergine sky as it descended. After a few moments, the strong wind stopped and the halo hovered over the crater hole, like a spaceship preparing to land.

Hattie, Peggy Pigeon, the Brummie Chickens and Dr Vynegarr burst into the Chamber Lounge, clambering over Missie and The Mice Boys. They stopped in their tracks, when they saw the floating halo. It shone so brightly, making it difficult for them to see.

Hattie felt a tingling in her back, so she shuffled her shoulders from side to side. She felt like she was being tickled under her arms. The tickling became more intense as gold glitter began to disperse from her shoulders. The glitter looked like a display of sparkles after a firework had popped. The gold glitter gradually began to form into the shape of wings which pushed through Hattie's dungarees, illuminating the Chamber Lounge. The wings moved gracefully inwards and outwards, until they began flapping in a rhythmic pattern. Hattie's feet started to lift from the floor. Shifting her weight onto her tippy toes, she floated upwards in the Chamber Lounge.

Everyone stood still and gawped at what they were witnessing. They were so captivated by this supernatural spectacle, they barely noticed the four electric blue-haired rabbit porters entering through the Chamber Lounge door, carrying shiny gold trumpets. Usually they entered through the ground which caused astronomic holes in Hattie's garden but this time, Hattie was in their home.

Although they were unimpressed by the pieces of discarded chicken scattered around the room - they were so Very Very Vegan after all, they filled their lungs with air and blew into their trumpets,

DUH DUH DUH DUUUUHHHHHHH

DUH DUH DUH DUUUUHHHHHHH

The blue haired rabbits lowered their trumpets and with one hand behind their backs, they hollered,

"BY THE POWER INVESTED IN US BY THE GALAXY GARDEN, WE INDUCT HATTIE MAE JAMES TO BE THE HALO BEARER, *AGAIN*. ALL HAIL, HER GALAXY GARDEN MAJESTY, HATTIE MAE JAMES!"

Everyone cheered, except Booker, Dlux and Gartoid. They had no idea what was happening! They watched as Hattie ascended further towards the halo, her angelic glow reflecting like a lighthouse over dark seas.

33
Through the Crater Hole

After a while, Hattie slowly began to descend. She smiled and reached out her left hand towards Man Like Dlux whose claws had lifted from the ground slightly. He was guided gently through the air towards Hattie and placed on the coffee table.

Hattie reached out her right hand, as a dazzling light appeared, forcing everyone to cover their eyes. She caught the light and lowered it gently as it gradually became dimmer. To her surprise, she noticed someone was standing by Man Like Dlux. The halo had matched him with a woman!

Hattie grinned with excitement as she saw Man Like Dlux's beak quivering. He began to cry.

"Babes..." he muttered with sadness in his voice.

"My dear Dexter!" The woman cried out.

They hopped towards each other and hugged passionately.

"My baby. My dear baby Dexter," the woman said, smiling at him.

"I've been looking for you everywhere, babes. Yo peeps, this is my wifey, you know!" He put his arm around her shoulders to show her off.

"Fellow Galaxiers and *guests*," Hattie interrupted, glaring at the uninvited Gartoid, "the halo has reunited... Man Like Dlux with his wife."

The Galaxiers, the Wonder Warren Rabbit Team and Booker, started applauding and wolf whistling to celebrate the happy occasion. Gartoid who was watching from the corner, gradually became more agitated,

"Hang on a bit. Hang on a bit!" He yelled, "yuh see dis here? This is *my* halo you know! Gi me back

NOW! I knew this likkle girl here had something to do wid dis. Yuh likkle thief! I said, gi me back!"

When he realised he was getting nowhere, he lowered his voice and began to plead, pointing to the hovering halo.

"Listen to what I'm saying, just reach up yuh hand and pull it back fe me."

"I can't do that," Hattie chuckled.

"What you mean, man? Just reach out yuh hand, just reach out..."

"It's not possible Gartoid. The halo ascends back

into the sky once its united the animals. See?" Hattie pointed at the halo as it gradually floated upwards and disappeared from sight.

"What? A joke yuh a run?" Gartoid said as he scrambled onto furniture to chase after the halo. He pulled himself up onto a breakfront cabinet and from there, he leapt onto one of the edges of the crater holes. His legs swung from side to side as he tried to hold onto the grass to launch out into the garden. Everyone was silent as they watched him struggle to pull himself up. AWKS! He gritted his teeth and cried out in pain, as he forced his body upwards.

"Aaaaaahhhhhh" he screamed, as he finally rolled onto the grass.

"Come back! Mi sey COME BACK," he shouted while running after the halo which continued to ascend into the sky.

"The Queen needs yuh...." His voice became a distant echo as he continued to chase the halo.

"Well done, Hattie," Peggy said, smiling, as she held onto Dlux's hand. "You did it, darling! I'm so happy! This reminds me of when we first met. Do you remember? You couldn't get through the wall of roses to meet my friends at Rosebush HQ but you persevered dear. Even when your hands were on fire, you still tried to save the plants you set ablaze. Hattie, I've seen you do this again and again.

Do you remember what I said in the elevator? We all get lost sometimes, but when we continue to be kind and compassionate to others, and to remain open to possibilities, we *eventually* find a place where we can belong. And, look! You've got it all here. *Never* forget Hattie, you have something very special inside of you. You have a superpower and it isn't the halo. Your superpower is simply being *you* dear!"

"WOW Peggy!" Hattie exclaimed.

"Wow indeed! I've watched you apologise when you realised you were wrong; that's commendable. Although you were not obliged to give Missie Mouse and her friends food, you still fed them. I know that didn't work out too well as Neville ratted everyone out, but that shows me you were trying to be kind. Now you recognise the value of helping others with the added bonus that you're the halo bearer again. I believe this shows your desire to be the best person you can be. Not just for the Galaxiers, but more importantly, for yourself. *That's what leaders do Hattie!* We need more little girls like you, who keep striving to achieve the end goal, no matter the challenge. I'm very proud of you Hattie. Your destiny has a sound and you've followed it here to your home."

Hattie was curious, *"my destiny has a sound?"* She'd never heard that phrase before.

"Yes, dear it does! All you have to do is listen. It will *always* lead you home." Peggy stopped. She realised that everyone was watching and listening.

"WELL" she heralded, "what are you all staring at me and Hattie for? It's bashment time! LET'S PARTY! We're having a Pigeon Banquet ALLLLLL NIGHT LONG!!!!!!!"

Hattie was speechless. Her parents had always told her how special and beautiful she was, but she'd never heard anyone else say it like *this* before. It made her feel like she belonged. This *was* her new home after all.

"Hold on! What about your speech? We always have a speech when we get a reunification Peggy." Missie Mouse said sidling up to Peggy.

Man Like Dlux interrupted, "yo, turn the music on fam!"

34
Yo! What You Saying Fam?

Missie Mouse needed no further invitation.

"Let's have a Pigeon Banquet!" She screeched, ran to the

sound bar, switched it on and turned the volume up so loud, that the Chamber Lounge walls vibrated with each beat.

The Mice Boys (now steady on their feet) burst through the door, ripped open their double-breasted jackets, threw them on the floor, and started shaking their hips to the music.

Some of the rabbits busied themselves clearing up the remains of the chicken giblets from the floor. Others, did a hoppity skippity dance in formation, jumping from one foot to the next. Dr Vinegarr nodded her head to the beat of the music and Booker stuck to his usual two-step moves whilst munching on the remains of his baguette. He didn't see them coming, but a few of the Wonder Warren Rabbit Porters marched over to him, with steam coming out of their bunny ears. A very uneven game of see saw then ensued. Booker gripped his beak onto one end of the baguette and the Wonder Warren Rabbits planted their feet in his jaws, trying to wrestle it from him. There were more of them than Booker, but he fought them off with his wings until they ended up like a stack of falling cards with their legs in the air.

In the meantime, Missie Mouse ordered more vegan food from the porters. Everyone danced, drank juice and enjoyed the celebrations until—

" O M G   O M G OMG," Missie shrilled, pointing to the crater hole as she jumped up and down.

"Look! It's the Afro Bees! - all three of them."

She toddled over to them and asked, "where have you been guys?"

"The RSPCA didn't catch us, so we stayed back and helped some of the others."

"The others?" Missie enquired. Suddenly, a

familiar male voice blubbered, "Oye oye!!!"

Hattie screamed with excitement. It was Howard Horse.

" 'Ows about that? Someone's 'aving a good time! Who's been matched then?" Howard Horse asked.

He galloped into the Chamber Lounge through the crater hole with some of the remaining Galaxiers on his back. They all slid down his hind legs and joined the Pigeon Banquet.

"It's Man Like Dlux and his wife, Peggy Pigeon." Hattie explained to Howard Horse. "They've been matched."

"Man Like Dlux? That roughneck! She picked 'IM? Well, doh ray mi; I've been to his rap shows before, kiddo. Bit of a show-off that one. He's 'ad a bit of plastic surgery recently. 'Is eyes are BUTCHERED to smithereens! Sack the pigeon surgeon. That's what I say!

Anyway, glad to see you back halo girl! Cuz last time I saw ya, you were on the frog and toad in Islington. Remember? When you refused to 'elp me friends? I thought you was a right artful dodger. I couldn't believe it!

But a dicky bird told me you went to Vinnie's to find me, so you could 'elp the Galaxiers after the RSPCA raid. I thought Gordon Bennett, you're a good dustbin lid ent ya! You recognise your mistakes and try to put 'em right. Not many people know 'ow to do that. I respect that and I'm proud of ya treacle. Glad to see you back now halo girl! Anyway, show me to the food platter, 'Attie."

The room was now full of Galaxiers partying. Hattie was so happy to see everyone again. She hadn't forgotten though, that they still needed to come up with a plan to rescue the others from the RSPCA base. For tonight though, she would not worry about that, she would just celebrate Peggy's happiness. She watched as Peggy and Dlux wandered out of the Chamber Lounge, wing in wing.

"I've got a present for you babes." Man Like Dlux's veneers glimmered as he handed his wife a gift.

"What is it, dear?" Peggy asked.

Using her wings - so she didn't get her nails chipped, she opened up the gift.

"Oh sweet baby Jesus, it's my Golden Love Bread! Thank you Dexter. Where did you get this?" Peggy asked.

"Don't worry about it, yeah? Just know that I love you. I'm glad I've got you in my arms again, babes. I never stopped looking for you, you know."

"Me neither. Oooohh come here, my love." They hugged and kissed each other.

Hattie walked over to them, "c'mon guys, it's performance time. Are you in?"

Man Like Dlux laughed, "ARE WE IN? Do you know who I am, sis? I'm the Pigeon Papi out 'ere. Ain't dat right, babes?"

Peggy Pigeon nodded and smiled and they both headed to the stage. They performed a rap duo while breaking into their old school moves. The Pigeon Banquet was now a Pigeon Bashment. Most of the Galaxiers didn't know Peggy had that kind of rhythm in her feathers.

The Mice Boys and The Afro Bees had a dance-off, and even Missie Mouse gave singing a try, testing everyone's tolerance. They chatted and laughed and listened to each other's stories, about what they did when they became separated and how the Galaxy Garden has given them a place to belong.

Hattie was so happy for Peggy Pigeon and Dlux. Peggy had worked so hard; she deserved this moment. Hattie followed them as they were heading outside.

"Where are you guys going?" Hattie asked.

Peggy Pigeon turned to Hattie and replied, "my dear, never you mind."

"What about the Galaxy Garden Peggy, when are we going to rescue the others?"

Man Like Dlux said, "so what, Hattie? We're done with that, now we have each other."

"What?" Asked Hattie.

"It's been a pleasure, dear, but now I've got my pigeon Papi, I've got to go and rebuild my city. I have to at least try to get it up and running; my people need me. Dr Gertrude Vynegarr will have to take over the Galaxy Garden. Remember what I said Hattie, be kind and compassionate and stay open to possibilities dear."

Hattie was taken aback. After all Peggy had said about friendship and loyalty, she was now flying away within an hour of reuniting with her husband.

"But—" Hattie started to say.

Hattie watched as they hopped from the ground and launched into the air. They flew over the Chamber Lounge at speed and disappeared out of sight as the

Pigeon Banquet celebrations continued. No-one else noticed they'd left. This time Dlux's sliders remained firmly on his feet.

What was the Galaxy Garden going to do without its matriarch now? How would she tell the Galaxiers that Peggy had abandoned the group without saying goodbye? A flood of tears streamed down her face—

"Hattie?" sounded a voice from a distance.

"I've been looking for you everywhere! Your mum brought me here to surprise you, as it's the last weekend of the summer holidays. She said you were playing with Shanti next door; I went there, but they're out. So I came looking for you in the garden."

She stared at her surroundings with curiosity then asked, "Hattie, what are you doing down there? How did this massive crater hole happen? And, why are you talking to animals?"

It was her best friend, Mia. But how long had she been standing there?

It's coming…

Visit: www.halohattie.com

Come say hi on Instagram & get updates at: @halohattieauthor

Halo Hackers!

Be a HALO Hacker! Get involved in social activities, whether it's art work, photos, leaving book reviews or joining us on social media. We love, love, love to hear from our readers AND we read *every single email!*

Check out the activities below and come up with your own. Paint me a picture, or find a creative way to show what you enjoyed about the book! Be a **Halo Hacker** and send all your entries to: **halohattieteam@gmail.com**

LA Edwards

Author Spy Cam
Guess what is true or false

Islington is one of her favourite places
She is an only child
She received grade E for GCSE Spanish

She had pet mice

She enjoys banquets

She has met author,
Malorie Blackman

She has a
friend with the
nickname Dlux

She eats pavement chips

Favourite Character

Draw your favourite character from the book in the box below and tell us why you like them. When you're finished, send it to us. You may get featured on our social media pages!

Mice Banquet

I'd love to hear your ideas for Missie Mouse's next Mice Banquet. Describe or design her next banquet, right here! Send it to us. You may get featured on our social media pages!

Halo Hattie Character Phrases

Peggy Pigeon
"Girl, I don't get my nails chipped?"

\-

Gartoid Manderblythen
"Unu, unu, unu, unu unu AND UNU"

\-

Brummie Chickens
"0121 and do one!"

\-

Auntie June
"Fire Fire, HotHot, Chilli, Sizzle, Razzmatazz, Sass Crisps"

242

T-shirt - Character Phrase Design

Pick your favourite character phrase from the previous list and design it on your own t-shirt. Send us your entries. We'd love to see them!

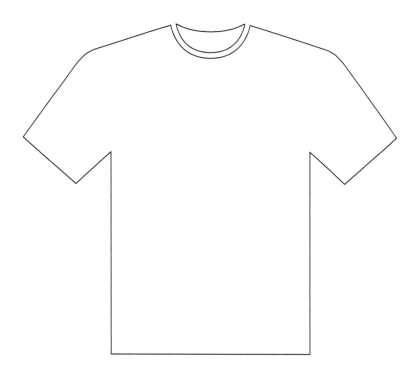

Poster - Character Phrase Design

Pick another favourite character phrase from the previous list and write it in the box below. Then, design your own poster by drawing what you think your favourite character looks like. Don't forget, send us your entries!

Spy Cam Loading...

Meet the Author

There are many references throughout Halo Hattie that relates to her real life. Get your batteries ready to charge your spy camera to find the answers on the next page.

Final Word from the Author

I started to write this book 10 years ago whilst at University. I enjoyed my degree, but I didn't feel fulfilled. So, I started forming ideas for a children's book.

Once I graduated, I soon became overwhelmed with work responsibilities. I lost my sense of creativity; but every now and then, I would return to writing but ad hoc writing wasn't enough. So, I quit my job! Eeek! Everyday for months, I would write, edit and re-write, but I still didn't finish my book but in the end I had to return to work.

Five years later, my family had two sudden bereavements. Their passing made me realise that I could be too late to reach my goals, or even finish Halo Hattie. I therefore decided to balance work and commit to finishing this book (again). It's been a rollercoaster journey but it's here!

So far, my soft book launch in July 2021 - sold out! I've had offers for Halo Hattie to be stocked in independent book shops, local libraries and I've received excellent feedback from parents and children with requests for a sequel. But, it doesn't stop there!!

I had the wild idea of curating a full cast for Halo Hattie, the Audiobook! I reached out to fellow peers, celebrities and actors who loved my outlandish idea and said - YES!!!

This was beyond my expectation! It continued to serve my mission to increase the presence of black representation in children's fiction. Yes, I'm only one person but, I'll be honest - I don't care. If it makes a difference that's a win :-)

It's important to note that, all professionals who helped bring this book and audiobook to fruition are from the black community. I'm very proud of that! Even if it is my name on the front cover, in my view, it is a community effort!

I say all of that to say this...no matter how long it takes you - commit to the gifts God has given to you. He will make provisions for the vision! Your destiny has a sound...That's all folks. Ya'll stay blessed now, you hear!

LA xx

- Islington is one of her favourite places

Yep. Good memories!

- She is an only child

True!

- She received grade E for GCSE Spanish

Unfortunately true! I missed the written exam. Eeek!

- She had pet mice

Absolutely not!

- She has a friend with a nickname, Dlux

Although that would be pretty cool. Nope!

- She has met Malorie Blackman

This is true! I still have the original copy of Malorie Blackman's Thief! Ms Malorie kindly signed it and told me to 'finish your book!' Here I am, years later, with Halo Hattie - Thanks Malorie!

- She loves eating pavement chips

Really??? I hope you didn't tick this one...you did, didn't you?

Listen to your favourite characters come alive with a full celebrity cast!

Visit: www.halohattie.com

Come say 👋 on Instagram & get updates at:
@halohattieauthor
Halo Hattie merchandise coming soon

Get featured on the website!
Colour in Hattie and email it to me!
I'd love to see it.
Get colouring :-)